SILVER MOON

GREAT NOVELS
OF
EROTIC DOMINATION
AND
SUBMISSION

NEW TITLES EVERY MONTH

www.smbooks.co.uk

TO FIND OUT MORE ABOUT OUR READERS' CLUB
WRITE TO;

SILVER MOON READER SERVICES;
Barrington Hall Publishing
Hexgreave Hall
Farnsfield
Nottinghamshire NG22 8LS
Tel; 01157 141616

YOU WILL RECEIVE A FREE MAGAZINE OF EXTRACTS FROM OUR EXTENSIVE RANGE OF EROTIC FICTION ABSOLUTELY FREE. YOU WILL ALSO HAVE THE CHANCE TO PURCHASE BOOKS WHICH ARE EXCLUSIVE TO OUR READERS' CLUB

***

NEW AUTHORS ARE WELCOME

Please send submissions to;
Barrington Hall Publishing
Hexgreave Hall
Farnsfield N22 8LS

Silver Moon books are an imprint of Barrington Hall Publishing which is part of Barrington Hall Ltd.

Copyright Richard Carradine 2010
This edition published 2010

The right of Richard Carradine to be identified as the author of this book has been asserted in accordance with Section 77 and 78 of the Copyright and Patents Act 1988

ISBN 978-1-907475-62-7

All characters and events depicted are entirely fictitious; any resemblance to anyone living or dead is entirely coincidental

THIS IS FICTION. IN REAL LIFE ALWAYS PRACTISE SAFE SEX

TORMENTED PASSAGE

by

Richard Carradine

Illustrated by
'LOKI'

CHAPTER 1

I'd been well prepared for this, now reality, bizarre as it was, had arrived. I shifted on my high heels, feeling the plug work my butt. I'd been brought early to the bar and been lifted up and impaled on the dildo of the hook shaped mount. I was here now until I sold myself or the evening ended. If my nerve failed or I was lacking in attraction and I was left, literally on the hook, I would be taken off and punished by my trainer to encourage me for the next time. Being early had ensured that one of the best spots could be selected so I had to make the most of it. I was able to stand, half turned away from the bar, looking down it towards the door, watching the men enter.

The bar could have been taken straight out of the old West though the girls spaced evenly along the bar couldn't. I suppose that I, with my corseted waist, low neckline and knee length flared skirt, was as near as you could get. (Really though, I looked more like the ballerina on top of the music box, the mirrors all around helped with the illusion too, though no ballerina ever had a bust as big as mine!) Not so the other girls; they wore leather and latex. All the girls were held captive by the bar, some were cuffed to it by their ankles or wrists, others were collared to swooping light stands. The bar was long enough for twenty or so varieties of bondage. Mine was one of the less evident, if more extreme, forms of captivity. My trainer had placed me on a curved mount that came straight out from the front of the bar and the dildo plug secured on it was angled just right to keep me erect, even if the corset I wore had not ensured that! The swan neck of the mount disappeared through the folds of my skirt and, at first glance, I looked free of bondage. In truth, though, I could shuffle round it so I turned away from the bar or face up or down it but not look directly on to the bar. This little fact ensured that even though I could place one hand on the bar, there was no way I could get free. Not that any of the other girls tethered the bar could do that but depending where on the curved length of the bar or the type mount by which they were connected to it, they were limited much further in their range of movement or what they could see. Observing a likely prospect was everything. After, that is, ensuring you've the right approach. I took a sip of my drink, gathering courage.

My nerves were all of a jangle still. Anyone who looked at me knew just how I was secured to the bar. I could of course ask for help and get myself de-mounted but if I were to do that I would forfeit the mounting fee and that had another six days to run. I couldn't afford that. No, I had to be mounted to display my submission and availability. The evening had only just begun and, though nervous, I was determined to play it cool. Before ten, the girls had to do the asking, after ten the men could. Both parties could always refuse. Of course there were always the Grungies. I'd heard about them. I was told that they were not always easy to spot and girls had wasted a lot of time on no-hopers. My profile may well say that I'm a submissive masochist but even so I wouldn't like to spend too many nights on a hook waiting for Captain Right.

"Now don't rush it, girl. You've a lot to offer. Don't sell yourself short and be calculating. It's better to wait for the right destination with the wrong man than the wrong destination with the right man." Could I be certain I would know if he was the right man? And would I get the right destination? I'd memorised all I could but there were always new destinations coming along. I saw what looked to be my first possibility. He wore the uniform and the flash of a long voyageur. Good shoulders, slim hips and handsome features.

"Can I buy you a drink, Captain?" He looked at me with an appraising stare as though I was so much meat on the hoof and I felt uncertain but then he smiled and showed his white even teeth.

"I reckon you can, little lady. A single malt whisky!" I winced a little. I'd paid my trainer and, as I said, paid the bar for the mount plus a drinks allocation but if I bought too many drinks like that one and I didn't find a suitable berth quickly, I would be forced to take whatever I could get or spend another year or so earning enough money to take a second shot at this.

"Now you really are something!"

"Thank you, Sir. I see from your flash you're a long voyageur."

"Yes, darling. I'm scheduled for a run to Eden III so I'm out for a little shopping. And you look just like the sort of girl I'm interested in." It seemed ridiculous to blush when you're at a sellers bar, one specialising in female slaves, but then I have that sort of colouring and whoever said homo sapiens were a rational species ... Eden III, I thought, one of the prime colonies - and so good looking!

"I'm available, perhaps we could compare cards?" I shifted slightly, aware that the dildo was doing interesting things to my inside and that I was getting wet.

"Oh there's no rush, let's get to know each other a little in the old fashioned way first." His hand caressed one of my breasts. My outfit was so low cut that more than a hint of aureole showed and the slight jiggle imparted to my big breast made it threaten to spill out. It was a bit forward but then if he was shipping out soon he probably didn't want to waste time.

"Careful, Captain, I might pop out and black your eye!" I wasn't pleased at his presumption but made the awful joke and giggled anyway, sounding a bit bimbo-ish but at least managing to keep my annoyance concealed.

"I'll chance it, girl. You really are well developed. Are they real?" I felt a bit annoyed that he even had to ask because the choker I was wearing had my badge that confirmed I was genetically unmodified.

"Of course they are, there's nothing fake about me!"

"What's you particular bag then?" He made no apologies about his crass behaviour, but carried blithely on. "Masochism, bondage, water sports ... What?"

"Why don't we just compare cards and you'll know if we match." His hand was through the split in my skirt and the other was resting on my corseted waist. I only have a light dusting of pubic hair so little masked my pussy. The fat dildo filling my butt was of a size to make it pout out so he had no difficulty checking my labia or my clit.

"Uuuurrrrgggghhh!" It came out low and throaty and, as I jerked in arousal, one of my nipples did indeed pop into view.

"You really are a hot piece." He showed me the tips of his fingers, wet with my juices. "And what lovely teats!" He touched a damp fingertip to the jutting exposed nipple. "It must be all of two centimetres long. And you say it's natural?" He had the nipple between thumb and forefinger now and was rolling it from side to side, making me squirm and writhe on my impalement. "You are a naughty girl. Does this naughty girl like being spanked?" I felt my pussy tighten and I squirmed a bit more, "I'd keep you tied and tethered a lot of the time as well, whether you're naughty or not."

"Oh! Ohh! Ohhhh!" I was wriggling violently now, his fingers had found my clit and I was close to a screaming orgasm.

"Simpson, isn't it? I thought you were a short haul pilot. Inter system only? Do you know what the penalty is for taking advantage of clients of the Negotiating Room?" I heard him through a daze of pre coital excitement and felt angry at his interruption. But then the import of what he was saying got through to me. The Sales Bar is rarely called the Negotiating Room but that is its correct title. It looks like a bar so that people can talk and relate to each other under favourable conditions and non-outsiders are allowed in to view the proceedings. It's another area of profit for them, but outsiders aren't supposed to get involved with the girls. The penalty isn't so much legal recourse, though that is possible, they're guilty of fraudulent behaviour after all. No, no girl is going to risk delay in shipping out to take them to law. The Sales Bar bouncers, though, will beat a Grungy, an outsider who goes beyond voyeurism, to a pulp if they catch him but my trainer told me that doesn't always stop them.

"I really don't want to see you thrashed, Simpson, so I'll give you a head start before I point you out to them on the security camera." The man who had called himself Captain Simpson almost snarled but also looked as though he might wet himself and suddenly his hand left my crotch and he literally ran from the bar.

I felt almost in shock, so bereft and let down by the turn of events. I looked at one of the mirrors on the wall across from the bar. I no longer looked like the figure on top of the music box that I had seen when my trainer had first impaled me on my mounting. My waist was still about forty centimetres, it's hard to ruffle a corset and my skirts flared out wide to further emphasis it but my large breasts had escaped my bodice and my hair looked a mess.

"May I introduce myself? I'm Captain Avon of the 'Sweet-Thing!'" I looked at him for the first time. He was slightly above medium height (if I hadn't been wearing shoes that kept me on my tip toes my head would have only come up to his chest) trim and well muscled but not too much so. His face was almost handsome in an unimaginative, almost non descript way. Still quite young, he nevertheless had the aura of certainty that said, 'I will endure' - the motto of the long voyageurs. "This is my first visit to a Negotiating

Room, they didn't have them when I first took my ship out." I did a swift double take.

"They've been established nearly two hundred years now."

"We compare cards, I believe." I stopped trying to get my breasts back into my dress and meekly offered mine. "Well, I am a long voyageur." He emphasised 'long', I did a quick sum in my head, even allowing for improvements in drive technology to minimise relativity's effects, he had gone a long, long way. I looked down at the card in his hand. My card and his now matched almost perfectly in colour. The small read-out showed zero point nine eight. I gasped and looked at him with fresh eyes. We were nearer than I'd believed or heard was possible. His hand slid between the flounced out folds of my dress and rested on my hips. "I like corseted waists," he indicated the still connected cards, "As you can no doubt guess. But I'm glad your hips aren't that big." He indicated the flair of my skirt, joking and, as he smiled and showed even white teeth, I found myself thinking how handsome it made him. "Such tight round buttocks." His fingers were exploring my cheeks now and just how big the plug that stretched and filled me was before going further. "Stockings! I dreaded the thought that these would have gone the way of the dodo!"

"I wear stockings all the time, sometimes rubber ones too. I also wear rubber tights so that the open crotch makes my cunt really pout."

"Delicious!" His head had gone down to one exposed nipple and he was sucking hard. It wasn't completely the done thing to be quite so blatant about fondling and playing with girls, even in a Selling Bar devoted to BDSM like this one but he knew that being displayed and humiliated like this was turning me on. I was coming again as his hand found the hard nub of my clit and this time there was no holding back.

"Eoooowwwww!" I came violently and the climax threatened to go on forever.

"Well, slut, will you sign on?"

"Where are you going?"

"Quadrant Sixteen to System Proteus. It's where I went last time. This time we colonise."

I realised that it really would be a long haul. Nearly five years subjective time for me and no guarantee of a husband on arrival either. Most, if not all of the settlers would have partners. He too would have no one to take up my berth for the return journey if I stayed, though. I looked at our still locked cards. This really was the wrong destination with the right man. I had to be calculating, my trainers said. I pressed my thumb on the sensor circle of his card then watched as he thumbed the circle on mine. They fell apart but stayed the same colour. Mine now said, 'The property of Jude Avon, Captain of the Star ship 'Sweet Thing!'' and his said, 'Owner of Ginny Dunlop, Slut and Sex Slave'. As I said, Homo Sapiens are not rational creatures.

"Open wide." He took the ball gag from his pocket and offered it to my mouth. "We might as well start as I intend we go on." I opened my mouth to protest that taking things slowly might be just as nice but then it was in and the strap buckled behind my head.

"Ungh!" Protest was obviously not going to be an option. The cuffs and harness were clearly the latest folding items for they hadn't made more than a slight bulge in the pocket of his dark blue uniform jacket, though I was pleased to notice that the same could not be said of his trousers. He definitely had a truncheon to go with the cuffs. Right wrist was cuffed with a metallic click and my arm folded up behind me. Left arm was cuffed around my bicep and the token struggle confirmed I wasn't going to bring my arm down, for a short rod, similar to the cuff and rod arrangement I could see in his other hand, connected them. This second device disappeared from sight quickly and now my left wrist was cuffed and connected to my right upper arm. I could flap my pinioned arms but I couldn't bring them forward or lower my wrists. I was helpless and available for anything he might want to do with me. I let the anal dildo ease a little deeper and felt my pussy involuntarily clench. The wetness already dampening my thighs increased and the cool air under my wide skirt helped raise goose bumps on my inner thighs, even in the warmth of the bar. Captain Jude was far stronger than he looked. He lifted me with ease off my impalement. He felt as strong as my trainer, though I knew that to be impossible. As I found my feet again, the weirdness of starting to live my fantasies hit me. I could feel my bottom still agape from the plug. Before my sphincter tightened it felt as though a dildo of air was filling me, chilling my bowel in a ghostly reminder of the dildo plug's presence. I don't think I had ever been quite so conscious of the sexual potential for pleasure of my butt and cunt.

It had been a big plug, I thought, as I watched the sconce-like arm disappear into the bar to be readied for the next girl who wanted to sell herself to a Captain of a colony ship for the long voyage. It would have been nice to have the sort of money that would have enabled me to go as a full colonist rather than as a supernumerary, or would it? Unthinking, I shrugged and my nipples popped out of my bodice again.

"Eeeeww!" I moaned to attract his attention and shook my tits at the Captain as he was busy untangling a lead and hadn't noticed. He turned me round so my back was to him and, reaching over my shoulder, cupped one big tit and scooped it back under cover then re-located my other breast.

"As we're still on Earth, I think we should be a little more decorous." I wasn't sure if he was being serious or not but I felt indignant. It was his cuffing me that made fall-out inevitable at some point. The collar was around my neck and he began to lead me from the bar. The cloak I wore to cover my outfit when my trainer escorted me to the bar was still in the cloakroom but now there was no way I could tell him that. The eyes of the buyers and grungies were on me and I could feel their lust, it was both frightening and arousing. The other prospective slaves looked on and in them I could see envy. It wasn't unusual for a girl to be chosen on her first night and just as quickly as I had been. To my eyes, many of the girls were as pretty or even prettier than me but they had to wait for the right combination of destination and compatibility. I had decided on only one guideline - sexual compatibility. Most were waiting for the right destination too; the majority would have to accept some sort of compromise before their bar fee ran out or they could try another time after they'd saved more money, just as I would have done had the Captain not come along.

I watched Captain Jude Avon's back as I followed him towards the door, trying to minimise the jiggling of my tits so they didn't fall out again, not easy with the tall heels I wore and my hands cuffed. I faced four or five years' subjective time as a toy to a possible maniac with the knowledge that there was no going back because, long lived as we now are, my parents would be long dead by the time I returned. Was it so important to be able to have as many children as I wanted, away from crowded Earth? It hit me again, even as the ache built in my ball gag jacked mouth. I had let my erotic fantasy lead me rather than common sense. It was a long way away and it was a new colony; perhaps I wouldn't be able to find a husband. A lot of colonies, because of the need to up the birth rate, practised polygamy. It might be a colony that was old fashioned and practiced monogamy so I wouldn't be able to become a second wife.

As we went through the doors into the real world I saw the eyes of passing pedestrians lock on to me. I glanced down at my near bare breasts and I could see a semi circle of aureole peaking over the top of my bodice again. They were only stopped from bouncing free by the hard erect stubs of my nipples. I'd had a love-hate relationship with my boobies since they first began to develop; I'd gone from flaunting to hiding them many times as I matured. Now concealment of any kind was in my Master's hands. A droplet of saliva dripped from my wide jacked open mouth and added to the sheen building on the firm flesh. Never have I felt so helpless and humiliated; my fantasies had included being displayed but this was reality. This was a total stranger leading me out on to a public street at the end of a leash. I had sold myself to him to use as he might want and whilst Earth side, I had forgotten to ask how long he would be earth bound, my condition would be evident for the world to see. The voyage could be even worse, for the term of the journey he could do anything that he wanted to me and there was nothing I could do about it. True, the whole voyage would be taped and that would preclude my life being at risk, other than from the voyage itself and thousands of frozen colonists would share that. No, it was that, my fantasy or not, I had agreed to enslave myself to a stranger who might just have found a way round the compatibility card. A teenage boy looked at me, we made eye contact and I shuddered at the vicious lust I saw in them. Sudden depression hit me and fear built up, I felt as though I would wet myself. No juices of excitement flowed now and I felt my pussy contract.

It was a summer evening and though almost nine o'clock it was still light.

"Slut!" It was an older woman wearing the black dress and headscarf of a religious fundamentalist who passed us as Captain Jude hailed a Jitney cab. Not everybody was happy about the sexual openness and trading of favours that was the mark of this century. People like that rude crow couldn't get their head round the fact that, with disease by and large beaten, people could trade and use their sexual talents in the same way as in the past an athlete had used his or hers. Of course that was the reality of our Earth-side society. Personally, though, I flushed to the roots of my hair, the fear that filled me didn't stop that. Getting used to being a slut and sex slave isn't easy and it might be my compatibility card that was screwed up and not his. Embarrassed I might be but she was right, it's what my card said. I felt humiliated yet I found it exciting too. Revitalised in an instant, my mood swung up again. I looked around at the Tri-D images that had started to become more vivid in the softening light. The upper levels of the tall buildings around us had the angled reflective surfaces that stopped these man-made canyons from being in a perpetual gloom but now, with fading light, the evening would become almost claustrophobic with the number of interactive advertisements intruding in your life. You could walk right through them even as they gave up their message to your ear but at night it became worse because they gained a spurious reality in the dimming light. They added the sensation of manic motion to the crush filling the streets twenty four hours a day. Was this the sort of environment that I wanted to live and bring children up in?

A Jitney cab drew up and the Captain made me climb in. It was the first time in this type but I suppose I should have tried it sooner. The rank this one came from was obviously aimed at the clientele of that Selling Bar and it opened my eyes to what might be to come more than any trainer could. New alloys and ultra carbon fibre ensured that the Jitney was not only light but the mechanism was as near friction free as made no difference. It needed to be because the girls pedalling it were to pull the both, Captain Jude and I, a considerable distance and up one or two steep hills. Of course, in by-gone days everyone assumed that powered mechanical devices would take over all hard labour. Daft really in a world approaching bursting point. We can't let people starve and there are so many of them they might as well work. Especially criminals, why let them sit on their backsides when honest people are working to feed them? Oh, in most cases where the work is dangerous to health and safety or where consistency is ultra important, machines do the work. But that still leaves a lot of things that people can do as well if not better than machines, if of course a degree of unreliability is acceptable. For instance, the controller in the Jitney is a bot, it needs to be precise and emotionless to fulfil its role properly. I challenge a human to be unemotional. In appearance it looks like a ventriloquist's dummy but only because it doesn't warrant the effort to make it look realistic, the casing is after all only window dressing. It's the ponies that command the attention anyway. The head's quite handsome in an androgynous way, it doesn't have the macabre overtones of the dummy and, though the half body with its arms holding the reins is out of proportion, they're still shapely and pleasing to the eye. The ponies were pleasing to the eye too, two female convicts, (pony-girls used for public transport are almost certainly criminals of some sort under punishment, though because this was a private cab specialising in the BDSM trade they might not have been.)

"Where to, Sir?" The bot was clever enough to recognise gender.

"The Whipping Post Hotel." I felt a frisson of excitement as my slave slut life was about to start in real earnest.

With my hands pinned behind me between my shoulder blades and my mouth plugged I could do nothing except lean back into the upholstery and accept what was to come. I felt, for the first time, the freedom that total abrogation of freewill gives to a slave and it was curiously peaceful. His hand slid through the opening in my skirt and found my pussy, automatically, as though I had been a slave forever, I opened my thighs to make myself more accessible. My breasts had bounced free again and this time he made no effort to replace them; instead he began to suckle my teat.

"Ahhhh!" It was the only coherent sound the gag allowed me. For an instant I closed my eyes and revelled in the sensation. It had never been like this with the trainer. I opened my eyes again and looked past the bot cabby at the two muscular and well rounded female bottoms that rolled before us as they worked the pedals.

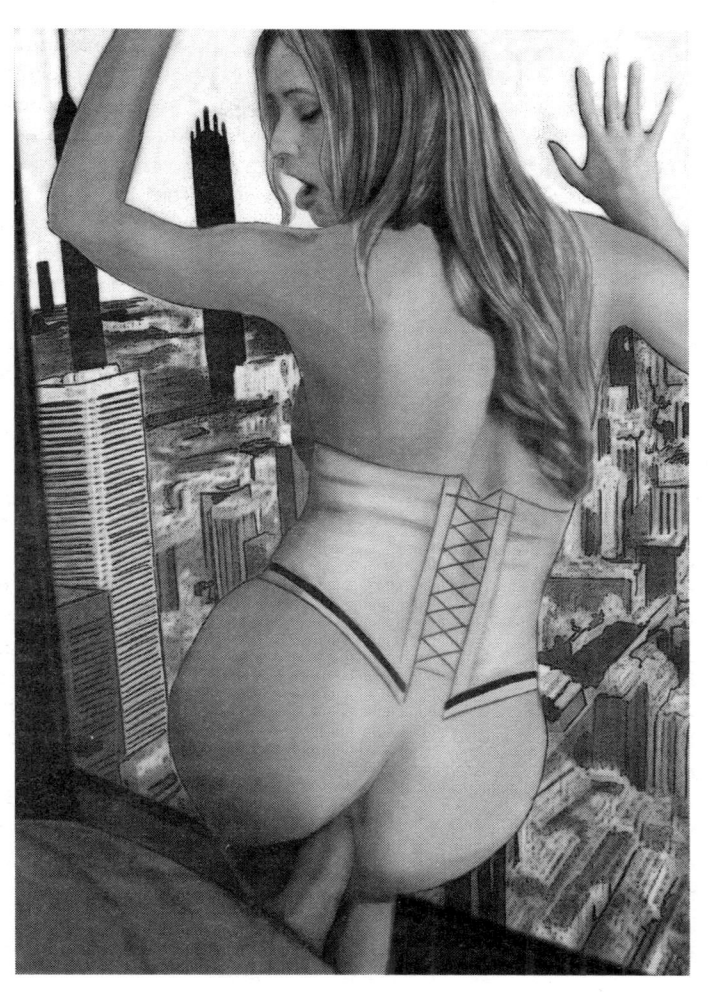

CHAPTER 2

The receptionist at the antique desk was blond, svelte and had two high apple-sized tits framed by her suit jacket and the collar of her white lined blouse. Neither was designed to cover her shapely little tits, more to display them and the brutally thick rings that pierced her dark stubby nipples. I stood there feeling horny, grubby and definitely sluttish as Captain Jude consulted with her. Before he could speak, she said. " I see you found what you wanted, Captain Jude?" She even had the cut crystal diction of the upper class and for a moment I hated her, then realised that we were sisters under the skin.

"Yes, thank you, Hot Slot." I blinked at this. Not so upper class then.

"You won't want my services tonight then, Captain?" There was regret in her tone.

"Probably not, but you never know."

"If you do, Captain, it would be a pleasure. I do swing both ways." Her eyes were hot on me and I felt myself flush. How could she, with another woman!

"I'll remember that." He started to turn away from the desk then remembered why he'd stopped off at her desk. "Any messages?"

"Forgive me Captain, there is ..." She swivelled on her stool and got up carefully. Within a short time of working with my trainer I had ceased to be surprised what women could take in their butts or pussies if they wanted to but even so I went wide eyed at its length and thickness. There was a glint of wetness on her bare fleshy and well-whipped bottom cheeks as they protruded through the open seat of her tight skirt. No definitely not upper class. She walked to a row of pigeon holes. It was all syncopated motion. The more expensive the hotel the more archaic they are. There was nothing archaic about Hot-Slot, she was slap up to date for this place. Returning to her seat she made a production of seating herself. I say a production but with a monster that big any girl would have to be careful. The Captain took the folded note and glanced at it as she sunk down with a liquid squelch.

"Fine. Should Captain Chin ring back let him know I'll be at the yard tomorrow around two. Oh and unless the hotel is on fire I'm not to be disturbed for anything." Miss Apple Tits Hot-Slot looked wistful and squirmed a little on her cunt filler but simply said.

"Yes Sir."

I followed him meekly into the elevator. It looked just like one of those creaky old lifts you see in old vids but even though it creaked convincingly I could still feel the G-force as it raced up the floors. He occupied a penthouse suite and as he led me into it, it became obvious money wasn't a problem. I suppose when I saw that it was a fetish classified hotel I should have realised that, old fashioned had disappeared and modern luxury was everywhere. Most long voyage captains aren't wealthy men and girls agree to take up their berths for new worlds and children, not money. Seemingly Captain Jude had both. A hotel specialising in a particular fetish or eroticism is always expensive. There are always people willing to work at their fantasy but not all are physically suitable. Anyone can be modified but it's expensive and if you have your employer loan you the wherewithal, you can find yourself locked into an employment contract for a long time. Still, lots do it for jobs or private contracts but it's for that reason, amongst others, that make this type of hotels expensive, as I said.

One wall of the main room was a huge Superglaz window - window? It was almost a balcony for the window folded and became a floor and you could actually walk out on to it. I stood looking down at the microlites diving and swooping in the up-drafts and currents around the towers. I didn't know what to do or expect so I just stood, not quite on the horizontal glass, watching the last of them stunting in the purple haze of the twilight as he made a call. I didn't hear him finish the call and suddenly arms encircled me. Automatically I moved forward onto the glass floor as hands cupped my breasts. Standing at that great expanse of glass I felt afloat in the purple light. It was as though I was outside my body looking at hands caressing and kneading breasts, watching my meaty teats being pulled and rolled between thumb and forefinger. Suddenly my skirt was pulled up out of the way and I was lifted and forced against the glass, my captured hands were tangled in my skirt and I could feel him hard against my bare ass. There was no way the Superglaz could break and let me fall and still that almost emotionless feeling held me tight yet in my mind I was floating free above the ground. He was in me, so big and alive in a way that my trainer never had, so vibrant and so demanding. My G-spot wasn't massaged, it was battered and reality flooded back. All that I had seen and experienced in the few short hours since being mounted and being brought here flooded in.

Confident or not of the Superglaz, even as I felt my body respond, the terror of falling took me, too. But that fear of falling and death only added to my arousal. I screamed into and around my gag and I came with massive mind numbing force as a lone glider swooped past the window, his eyes widened as he took in my tits pancaked and squashed against the glass. Then, as his eyes met mine and he took in the gag that spread my aching jaws, he stalled the glider and dropped like a stone. Just before I lost sight in the glooming darkness of the canyons between the blocks, the tumbling fall turned into a glide and he swooped gracefully away. He had regained control before the safety devices cut in but I guessed he didn't have enough updraft in the cooling air or light to come again and confirm what he'd seen.

In my warm post coital haze I wondered what fantasies the pilot would have before he slept. Or would he just be disgusted at a girl so obviously co-operating in her humiliation? No, I thought, he wouldn't have been swooping around this particular building if he was gay or straight, he would be horny as hell tonight I thought and found the thought pleasing.

I got my dress off easily enough after he released my arms and I was directed to the bathroom. The bidet with its dildo nozzle gave me pause for thought, though, as I struggled with the laces of my corset that my trainer had pulled so tight. It wasn't that I had any ignorance left as to why that particular accessory was fitted to the bidet, my trainer had ensured I was well scoured out before I was taken to the bar and mounted. No it was rather that this was to be the first time I was actually prepare myself for my own master. Rolling my corset up into a tube, I laid it on the vanity unit and looked at the honey gold complexion and full ruby lips of the girl who stared back at me with round amber eyes. Framed by thick black hair the face was mine, yet tonight I saw a stranger. A slut, a slave, a sex toy and a plaything, a creature without freewill. I shivered and trembled as a tongue flicked out nervously. That simple act and the sensation on my lips jolted the tape into synchronicity again and it was me once more. I began to sit, offering my sphincter to the jutting spouts. Physically it was bigger than I had experienced so far and mentally it was to be an act of collusion and affirmation of my new status. The bulbous head popped through my tight ring and I gave a low moan that none save I could hear. The special pain that only a virgin or near virgin butt can feel built but I carried on lowering myself down on the slippery material of the nozzle until I sat fully plugged and breathing rapidly, allowing the cramps to ease as I knew they would. My pussy pouted from the internal pressure and tentatively I touched my lips and clit. It felt like and electric shock and I could see my labia gleam wetly. I blushed, embarrassed at my own arousal.

The little control panel on the wall by my side had various settings but I chose standard. I could only take so much new experience. I couldn't wait for the initial discomfort of impaling myself to recede further so I pushed the button. For a few seconds my bowels received a chill flow but rapidly the water became blood heat and the cramping sensation started to increase again and fill my expanding belly. Unnecessary or not at this time to cleanse myself, it was baptismal. The water stopped automatically just at the point I thought I could take no more and the spigot began to slide from my butt. There was that popping sensation in reverse as it again broke through my sphincter and the fluid inside me was let go and I moaned long and low as a climax of confirmation took me. The bulbous head nudged my sphincter again, almost as though tasting me and for an instant it seemed as though it would fill me again but instead there was a chime and I looked at the control panel to see a display saying, "Ready for use." Somehow I knew it wasn't referring to itself and I blushed again.

Showered and refreshed, I stood before him clad only in hold up stockings and the high heeled bootees left out for me. My hands were clasped behind my back and my head meekly bowed. It was as much nervousness as the instruction my trainer had given me that made me show my submission. This stranger had bound me, displayed his mastery to the world, or as much of it as we had seen coming to this hotel, and fucked me. But for all our cards had seemed compatible, I hadn't exchanged more than a few hundred words with him at the bar and in the Jitney. Being used so had been beautifully sluttish and whorish and I'd found it exciting in the extreme but it still had an element of play-acting to soften reality. Reality was a well I was sinking deeper into as the minutes went by. This man now had total power over me. I was contracted to him and to break that contract was a criminal offence. I didn't want to end up pedalling a Jitney, to be used by anyone who wanted to pay for me. Punishment always matched the crime these days. If I broke my contract to submit, I would be forced into it and you could guarantee it would be submission to something I would hate. Within my contract I could rebel as much as I wanted, indeed if I suddenly discovered a dominant streak or I disliked him as a person so much I could fight him anyway I wanted. This was perceived as being part of the role into which we had both contracted but I couldn't walk away from him or ultimately refuse to interact with him.

"Let's have supper." His voice was soft and friendly as he indicated a seat at a table that had been set whilst we both showered and changed. Well, he had changed, stockings and bootees wasn't much of a costume, he, though, wore a one piece grey silk lounger that showed off his tight knit muscular body. I walked across to the round table, conscious of the bounce of my unfettered breasts and rolling bottom. I think all my cheeks blushed. He had an old world manner to him that I found disconcerting at first. He pulled out my chair for me to sit and the seat cupped and moulded itself to me. No dildo thrust at back or front, nothing buzzed or vibrated, it was more like the caress of hands that knew and loved me and as I shifted those hands would follow and stroke.

"Eeeeek!" The sensation disconcerted too but didn't displease me.

"Wine?" I was suddenly very thirsty and my throat dry. He watched me lick my lips and didn't wait for my verbal response. The wine, cold and dry, was like a lotion on my throat. "We seem to be compatible but this is all new to me so I think, Ginny, we need to get to know each other a little more than on an electronic level." Strangely I blushed and it was at that point there was a knock on the door. "Come!"

We live in times where we're all so much more open about the physical body and our fetish and fancies but it wasn't so long ago that I was a virgin living at home and, like most parents, Mum and Dad brought me up in a manner that educated me about sexuality but didn't confront me with it. At home I was dressed with a degree of modesty within the current fashions and I still wasn't sure what their particular eroticism or fetish was. In fact, like most children, I knew my parents were, but didn't actually believe they were, sexual animals just like the rest of us. Having been Psyche Profiled for the card I knew my own orientation but knowing and seeing the scene up close is something else. A man in an old-fashioned wing collar, coat and tails entered the room. He looked quite young, it's difficult to say how old people are these days. His hair was black as night and slicked back close to his head. A thin moustache lined his upper lip and his eyes had a hard glitter as they locked for an instant on my nudity. He clicked his fingers and two maids entered the room pushing trolleys. Both were clad in tight black rubber uniforms with white rubber frills. As they pushed, their full, bare and belled breasts hung free of their bodices and the skirts and aprons were so short that they showed bottoms and tight strapped pouting pussies, so tight strapped indeed that the straps almost disappeared between plump and swollen labia. When they straightened and stood awaiting their next orders, their mounds were exposed and the same strap bisected them and created twin humps where nature had given one. It was clear that the straps held plugs deep in them. They moved continuously on ballet boots that held them on point and because of this their legs were made to seem impossibly long and shapely in their tight black rubber stockings.

"It is all as Sir ordered but please call me immediately should anything not be up to standard."

"Thank you, Marcel. I will."

"Would Sir like the services of one or both of the maids?" There was no hint of accent in Marcel's voice. Most accents have disappeared but he probably was French. He looked French and his eyes, though trying to stay away from me, almost burnt my naked breasts and teats,

"Not tonight, Marcel. I would like to tip the girls, though."

"Of course, Sir." He carried a clipboard with him and he pressed something on it. In seconds both maids were holding on to each other so they could stay on their feet. Little maids' caps with white rubber ribbons dangling from them trembled with their shaking, surmounted heads that were hooded in black rubber, so tight that it was clear they were ball gagged. A small opening at their nostrils through which a ring protruded allowed them to breathe but the only other openings were for their eyes. Blank faced or not, those eyes made it clear they were both in the middle of massive orgasms. One of them began to scream and moan as well.

"Judy! Six demerits!" Immediately the other began to moan as well. "And for you too Suzy!" He pushed the button on his clipboard again and they both slowly calmed. He had sounded angry but I thought he was actually pleased. He waved his hand in a shooing motion and both girls left the room on legs that were now very uncertain. As they went I saw the shadows of crop marks across well-rounded and firm cheeks and I realised then just how their demerits would be paid for. The scene and the thoughts made me feel as though my pussy were going pulpy. "Enjoy you meal, Sir," he said and, with an almost eager step, followed them out.

I was shaken and excited by the scene played out but more than that I realised I was ravenously hungry. "Serve the meal, Slut." It wasn't said in a way to insult though in company it would have been one. It was what I now was and it excited me. I acted as maid, serving up the courses for us both. He caressed my bottom as I moved past or close to him and once slipped his hand between my legs to hold me as he checked my pussy. I froze, half expecting it and parted my legs a little more as I had been trained to do. "You're very wet, Slut." He held up three fingers that glistened and I blushed. He moved his hand again and I realised he was expecting me to clean them. I went scarlet. It was the first evening of my new life, embarrassment and degradation was becoming a permanent state but I licked him clean before drying his fingers on the napkin. He smiled at me, pleased with my submission and, for the first time, I realised how dark and deep his eyes were and felt weak. Here was a man who demanded respect and somehow, I knew, also one who could inspire fear.

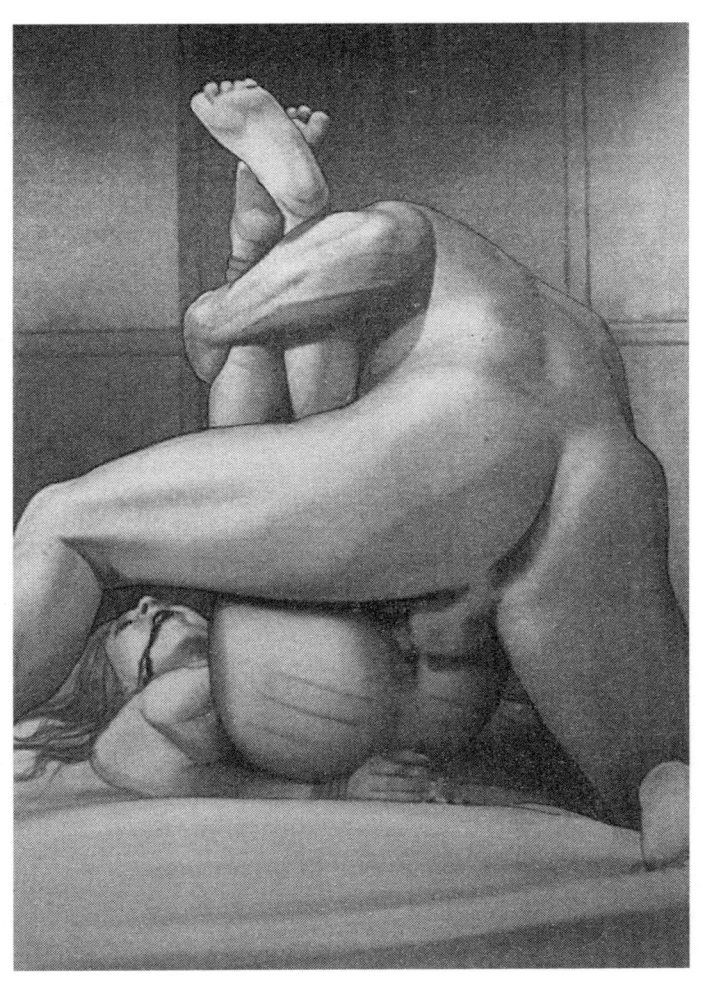

CHAPTER 3

It was as though I hadn't humiliated myself by being totally submissive. We sat and ate and as we drank we became easier with each other. He explained the technical side of the long voyage we were to undertake and we swapped backgrounds. His was far more interesting than mine.

"When I took my first long voyage I knew that I was leaving family, friends, the world I knew and that it was going to disappear forever. I suppose it was easier in one respect in that it had been something I had been working towards for five years. Possibly too the fact that my mother had died a year earlier, before the day I knew was coming but somehow felt would never arrive." He seemed to consider. " Yet when I think back, the fact that I was leaving a father to go on alone into old age, it was still hard. Of course I ensured that for the remainder of his life he would receive my salary until he died so I knew he would want for nothing monetarily but that was the least I could do. He encouraged me even though it was breaking his heart, saying, 'the chance to do and go where no other human being has done or gone is one you'll regret all your life if you don't,' he used to say that. 'I'd do it tomorrow if I weren't too old'.

"In the early days we relied on cryogenic suspended animation to get us through the voyages. Of course that still meant I had two years of subjective time to work through in both directions. You could only spend so long suspended before tissue damage started so you had to keep waking up and even in suspension you were somehow aware of the passage of time, if not fully conscious. You can always tell the 'old' long voyageurs by their eyes. They may look young as anyone else but they have time stacked up behind the lens of their eyes." I looked into his dark, dark eyes, saw the sadness and knew the truth of his words. "What makes long voyages hard to bear, as addictive as they are, is that you remember a yesterday so fresh and clear that to others is ancient history." For a moment he went silent and I realised that I had not only forgotten to eat but also to breathe. I thought of my own parents and tears filled my eyes. The conceit of youth made me wonder how they would manage without me but nonetheless I knew I would be missed, I was their only child. Any grandchildren they would have would be born hundred of years in their future, on another world and they would long be dust.

His tone changed as he shrugged off the weight of old sorrows. "It was on my second voyage that I discovered the Proteus System in Quadrant Sixteen. Of course because of the relative time period I was off Earth my back pay by this time was considerable and what with compound interest and finders' fee. I ended up a very rich man, if rootless and without family and friends or any sort of inter-relationship." He reached across the table and touched my nipple. I shivered at the loneliness he was describing. "This voyage I'm going out as Commodore of a fleet so I'll have other people in a mini society about me. And I'll have you," he added and I didn't know what to say to that.

"How come it's a fleet and not a single vessel?" The scenes I'd seen on the Tri-D of ships leaving Earth for the long voyage played through my mind, they always showed huge but single ships leaving or arriving.

"Planet three of the system is Earth-like in the extreme. Mineral rich and something like Earth itself must have been in the mid-Jurassic period. There are even dinosaurs of a sort, though apparently not of the size of T Rex!" He smiled at me and suddenly the stern Captain turned into a young man and I realised that in relative age that's just what he was. "So, as it 's so far away and such an attractive potential colony, a fleet of twelve vessels are being sent. And as I know the way," he laughed at his own feeble joke, "they put me in charge.

"Now what about you?" I considered what I could say to a man born hundreds of years ago, who had done so much, visited other living breathing planets and seen alien plants and animals.

"I wanted children, it's a lottery now even if the Pop Board would gives me clearance. The lottery came in after I was born, a few years later and I might never have been." I wondered how much of what I told him came under the heading of Ginny Dunlop or was it the social history of her time? "With life expectancy as it is there's getting less and less space for babies. Of course almost all dangerous sports are encouraged, even though they try to ensure they're not suicidal. All modes and manners of lifestyle are allowed so long as they don't hurt non-participating others or damage children." A sudden thought struck me. "Did they have the death penalty in your day?"

"They were talking about it."

"Well, the death penalty is the sentence for all pre-meditated murders. A few exceptions are allowed in cases where cruelty to the perpetrator has driven them temporarily insane. Rapists, child molesters, etcetera, all are liable to be put to death because they have forfeited their humanity." I had obviously allowed myself to become sidetracked.

"I brought myself up to speed on cultural changes in the slow down period of my last run home. How, though, have you got to where you are now?" I squirmed in the cupping caress of my seat.

"Oh, that's simple. Mum and Dad have a wonderful relationship but they're a long way from being rich. I want to have children. The odds of twenty to one for the lottery aren't good. I'm not clever enough to get the sort of degree that would guarantee me a place on a colony ship and they couldn't afford the passage money." I looked him straight in the eye. "Companions for long Voyageurs get a free ride and the odds of being taken up are better than the lottery, particularly if you have the little 'kink' that make you an attractive supercargo." I looked deep into those dark ancient eyes of his again. Their depth was reassuring not frightening. He gave a wry smile and I continued. "I had an inkling of what my sexual drive might be so I had a Psyche Profile done and it was confirmed." I looked down at my empty plate and blushed. "In spades it would seem!" I felt hot but carried on. "Mum and Dad took it well. Perhaps it's genetic and they're into the scene as well. Anyway, they hired a trainer for me and helped me get enough money to buy a space in the Bar. You know the rest.

"Was I your first lover?"

I flamed red again. "Is it important that I be a virgin?"

"No, it's just that it might make settling down to your new life more difficult if you're bringing baggage along, as it were."

"You were my first man." I felt awkward admitting that I'd never made love to another human being.

"What about your trainer?"

"Do psyche robots count?"

"Ohh!" He laughed. "That shows the gaps that occur in leaping the centuries. "I assumed that the trainer you referred to was a man. Or I suppose a woman."

"Uhhh! Gross!" I had contracted myself to him so he could use my body for transport to a new world. But to allow another human being I didn't have a relationship with or a contract in place to use me sounded like, like ... what was it they called it? Prostitution!

That night he collared me. It was an alloy band that fitted seamless and snug with rings so carefully inserted that they looked engraved. He rarely removed it. He popped a ring out from the flat surface and chained me to the bed head. I was aroused by the simple bondage and co-operated eagerly in his use of my body but that first night was taken slowly. We, as master and slave, had a long time to get to know each other.

He had bought me new outfit from the hotel to wear and bind me with. A black Slim Leather jacket that only covered my arms and shoulders and had straps that bound my body. The arms finished in fingerless mittens and when my arms were folded and strapped behind me I might just as well had no arms or hands. All I could do was wave my thumbs about to release the tensions that built in my hands. He had ordered me to use a depilatory cream so now I was as smooth and hairless as a newly born babe. The hairlessness increased too the stark definition of the straps that cut into my body, making my breasts swell and my mound bifurcate. Looking in the mirror, the end of the dildo, held in place by that slim tight crotch strap, filled the gap at the top of my thighs. Its stubby end was clearly visible for the world to see. He helped me into my boots and we were ready for the day. I went to ask him where we were going and I quickly came to realise that the seeming easy relationships we had started to develop had been for last night only.

"Don't speak unless spoken to. If you have to ask a question, ask permission first." I bit my lip and felt as though I were now in the presence of Mr Hyde as against Captain Jekyll. Oh that little device under the strap, I had been conscious of its presence ever since I had parted my legs to allow it entry. It wasn't that big but it was hard and unyielding and even now just only warming. "It has a proximity sensor fitted so that if you move to far from me, pain in that lovely pussy of yours will start to build." I bit my lip harder still and frowned. I had known that he might do anything to me and I also knew, if our cards had been right, that ultimately my body would take pleasure from it. What hadn't been evident or understood by me was that actually liking what was done didn't actually form part of the equation. I was learning rapidly. "It also has a punishment function. It can do this, if it's not appropriate to use this." He pulled a crop from a slim pocket in his uniform trousers and gave it a swish through the air, making me wince and blink. " And I can also do this." He pointed a ringed hand at me and suddenly a sharp pain filled my pussy that made me pull my legs together and crouch.

"Ooowww! You - " I never got to the bastard bit. Another pain filled me and I crouched even lower, only just managing not to drop to the floor and roll into a ball. It wasn't actually that bad but it had been unexpected.

"It obviously has different levels of pain and it can also do this." The vibration seemed to fill my whole body and now my knees were weakening for an entirely different reason. "So carrot and stick are two parts of its function. It also trains in another way, Slut." I could feel my juices running down my inner thigh over trembling muscles. "You have to keep squeezing it so that it starts to vibrate at this level." It dropped several levels of vibration and it was so low that it didn't bring on or threaten an orgasm. What it did do, though, was keep me feeling very pussy conscious, if not fruity. "If you don't keep your pussy muscles active and exercised, you can guess what will happen." He pointed the ringed finger at me again and I shook my head vigorously. I guessed just what would happen and I didn't want any of it.

I sat on a stool by his side as he breakfasted, feeding me also as he did. I could see other girls seated similarly to me with their masters or mistresses. Only one or two were long voyageurs. That was obvious, I suppose, not all long voyageurs are into BDSM, everyone has their own particular kink. Some Sales Bars, or rather Negotiating Rooms, are dedicated to homosexuals, some to just basic boring missionary position heterosexuals who want companionship rather than sex. Long voyageurs are as varied as anyone else. Many of the other sex slaves breakfasting were contracted to Terrestrial masters or mistresses for sex or money or both, I suppose. We attracted a lot of looks. Some I knew were for me but long voyageur Captains were celebrities in their own right. Just being here also told the world that Captain Avon, like the other Captains in the hotel, was also rich and successful.

At last we finished breakfast. I had been squeezing my pelvic floor muscles as hard as I could even as we ate. The pain had been held off but by now I was definitely oozing and my tummy ached with the effort. I was definitely into overkill and as he drank the last of his coffee I let myself relax. I may not be a brain but I'm not stupid either. I had to find out how the dildo controller had been set. I gave a hard squeeze, relaxed and began to count. One and two and three and four and ... the vibration continued until I reached forty-five then it stopped. I gritted my teeth and began to count again. One and two and three and four and ... Slowly and deliberately I counted the seconds. At forty-six the pain shot through me and as I gasped, automatically my pussy contracted and the buzzing started again. I was panting as I recovered from the sharp pain but felt pleased with myself. If I squeezed every minute or so I would ease the tension in my stomach from overworking the pelvic floor muscles and give myself a fifteen to thirty second respite from arousal. I had visions of climaxing long and loudly in front of crowd of strangers. The thought brought colour to my cheeks and I saw my master looking at me with a sly smile on his face. He knew just what I'd done and looked pleased with me but said nothing. I felt smug at my own cleverness.

"Now Slut, let's get things moving, shall we?" Just what things I didn't ask but scampered after him on my tall heels, keeping as close to him as I could. Masochism is one pleasure I can enjoy at the right time and place. Stupidity is never enjoyable.

A cloak was buttoned around me before I left the foyer. It came to just below the knee and though of fine black silk, was completely opaque, although it didn't conceal the shape of my swollen breasts or their jutting nipples. I was covered enough, though, so that propriety was maintained should we come into contact with children. With so few children being born on earth you didn't come across them on the streets that often but it was an etiquette for anyone fetish-y or erotically costumed not to go on the street uncloaked before nine at night. If broken it would attract strong public censure at the least and possibly a fine for an offence against public order if taken to extremes.

This time, the Jitney he hired was pedalled by two burly men and it was obvious that they were free and self employed Jitney cab men. No reins, no harness, no bot, noTri-V concealment, just a cab and pedal unit. "Where to, Guv?" I had the feeling that in ancient Rome you would have been greeted with a similar cry.

"The Lutterworth building." These were no girls forced to act as power source and flaunt their butts for fucking. These guys were fast, they just wanted to get to our destination as quickly as possible so they could collect a tip and get another fare. Their thighs and buttocks were muscular in the extreme, occasionally one or the other would glance in their mirrors to view me and my protruding teats and I found myself squeezing just a little quicker than necessary. I think they could see my arousal in my face. As we went through the door of the building Captain Avon took my cloak from me and even before I was out of sight of the cab his crop came down hard across my butt, making me squeal and jump.

"Naughty little slut. You going to make it hard for those two honest cabbies to pedal properly for some while." I was walking toward the elevators with the stubby end of my dildo on show and a livid red stripe across my cheeks. I couldn't see either but I knew all the straight suits around could and I was flame red again.

We travelled up with several other men and women. The lift was crowded and I could feel their eyes on me, one or two of the women in disgust but most of the men and some girls were hot and wanting. I could see which was which. As I made to step from the lift behind Captain Jude, hands fondled my breasts and cupped my butt, fingers pushing at the dildo I was still clenching.

"Eeeeek!" I glanced back at a sea of blank innocent faces. I felt a twinge of pain and realised that my master was at least thirty feet way from me and I scurried, tits bouncing and butt jiggling, after him. When I was near him again I turned and looked again at the lift. All those eyes were still watching me as someone had kept the doors open. I stuck my tongue out at them and went cross-eyed before following the Captain into an office.

"Doctor Khan?" The Doctor was big and blond with a beard and wore a turban. I wondered how many generations back was the original pure-bred Sikh.

"Captain Avon?"

"Yes."

"And this is obviously your slut."

"Indeed."

"Perhaps you would like to tether her and then come through to my office where we can talk without distraction." He sat me down on the floor and connected a totally OTT chain to my collar. It got worse because he then connected what I thought was the decorative strap around my ankle of my left leg to its companion on my thigh. I was held with one leg folded and unless I could figure a way of standing on one leg I had to remain sitting on the hard floor.

The door closed and I was alone, knowing they were going to be talking about me. For any woman this is an awful state to be in and for a sex slave of my type it is actually horrible. I shifted so I sat on my calves. That at least ensured my dildo was being pushed hard into me. It was strapped hard enough as it was.

"Hello!" I looked away from the door that they had closed between us and found I was looking at a white uniformed nurse. She wasn't at all fazed by my outfit or the fact that I was hobbled and chained. She was tall and her legs seemed to go on forever but they eventually turned into hips that were nicely rounded and full. Clearly she was corseted wickedly tight for her waist was tiny, making her huge breasts seem bigger still. Large green eyes stared out of a creamy white complexion that showed her overfull red lips to best advantage. A little white cap sat like a rowing boat on an ocean of red hair. A tongue licked out almost snake like showing a ringed and studded tongue. "Who are you?"

"G-Ginny Dunlop."

"Well G-Ginny Dunlop, I suppose you're just starting your contract?" Her voice was husky but kindly.

"Y-Yes." I hated myself for sounding so wet. "I've got a berth as supercargo on a long voyageur."

"I'm impressed, I've thought about it but didn't have the nerve, possibly they wouldn't have taken me either. I wasn't exactly prime genetic stock." I looked surprised at this beautifully erotic looking creature. "Instead I contracted to the doctor as nurse, model and toy for five years so I can get gene re-structuring. The women in my family are pretty homely, to say the least. I figured if I get re-structured I might get the sort of husband I want and might just end up lucky in the lottery." Whatever she originally looked like, homely is not what she looked like now.

"You look fantastic!" And she did. OTT but fantastic.

"Oh this is all cosmetic, nano-bot sculpted not gene related. Anyway I'm his mannequin, anything new or way-out he tries on me first."

"Is that why the Captain's brought me here? For modification?" My stomach went suddenly empty and cold.

"Probably but it could be for anything. You don't look as though you need much. Or have you been gene re-structured already?" She meant of course had my parents been gene re-structured.

"No, I'm badged as genetically unmodified." She looked impressed.

"I really don't know what he's got in line for you. Doctor Khan does specialise on the fetish side of medicine but it could just be for a confirmatory check up. There are girls out there with forged cards, you know." She looked down at me with a sparkle in her eyes and moved closer. "Would you like to see his mod catalogue?" I looked up at her, catching a glimpse of bare bottom cheek under her short skirt as I did so.

"Yes, all right." I watched as without any embarrassment she stripped off her short white button through uniform. I was mesmerised by the tightness of her corset and the size of her corset-cantilevered breasts. Teats of incredible size and thickness with bands of gold snug around their base adorned her huge but shapely breasts. As I watched she stretched and rolled her own nipples, showing just how hard her teats could be worked. Beads of fluid started to form.

"Want to try them?" A huge teat was dangled against my lips and somehow it seemed rude not to try. "Nip down on the gold band, they stop me from leaking and release the flow." It seemed all very clinical as though she were a mechanical drinks dispenser. A liquid bathed my tongue; it was delicious. A sudden jolt of my pussy made me bite down a little harder and suck in my breath and a jet of liquid filled my mouth. "My, you are an eager little thing," she said and almost dragged her teat from between my lips.

"Sorry, it was my dildo shocking me for not working it."

"Oh, don't worry, it felt quite nice really but I didn't want you to send me off." She straightened and parted her legs. Her clit was massive, swollen and ringed. Other rings adorned inner and outer labia. She seemed to breathe out and force herself to relax. I watched, fascinated, as a large black dildo slid from her pussy until almost eight inches was free of her sex. Suddenly she seemed to concentrate and I watched as, unaided, it slid hard back home into her wet slot.

"Arrrggggh!" It was sound of pure delight. "I know all about pussy control and training dildo. That big clit and my enhanced G spot keeps me multi-orgasmic and permanently horny all the time." Suddenly her long shapely legs were either side of my body and her ringed and engorged pussy was thrust at my face. "If you like the starter, try the main course." She thrust herself over my mouth and nose and I could do nothing save struggle to get free, my tongue fighting to clear my mouth of her wetness. For an instant I had been disgusted and then the taste of her hit me. She was delicious.

"Nurse Penny!" Suddenly I was free of her enhanced pussy and was panting for breath. She was struggling to tidy her uniform around her.

"I was just showing her some of the options open to her, Doctor."

"So I can see."

"I didn't get a chance to show her my bottom or my throat."

" Penny! Control yourself. Bring her in here. I'll deal with you later." I thought I could see a smile hiding under his beard. Penny didn't seem to put out and as she turned away her skirt had ridden up and I could see her butt was criss-crossed by fine lines of fading welts. If more of them were to come later, it didn't seem to bother her too much.

CHAPTER 4

No one had any doubt as to what I was at the dockyard but at least there was some degree of modesty to my outfit, spurious maybe but still modesty. The black Sim-Leather trousers I wore went seamlessly into the bootees with the heels that kept me on tiptoe. They were so tight that a goose bump would have shown. The trousers, of course, had no crotch, that was occupied with my dildo controller but if I was careful the pleated Sim-Leather skirt I wore over the top of my corset at least covered my pouting sex and my butt where it protruded through the open seat of the trousers. He wasn't being exactly kind in allowing this degree of freedom and modesty. We were outside the city and there was no climate control here. In fact we were so far outside the city that we'd had to take a government flitter to get here. No Jitney cab, no matter how muscular their thighs, could have got here in half an hour. It would have taken them a day. It was chilly and I could feel the goose bumps rise on the exposed parts of my body, particularly my pouting chest.

I know Sim-Leather was developed from space technology but it might as well have been developed for the terminally kinky too. In space you don't want loose flapping clothes catching on sensitive or even dangerous equipment. Nor do you want to bruise or cut yourself on the same equipment. It's easy enough to do that in an empty cabin when the gravity changes suddenly. Anyway, they developed this material that breathed like leather, was tough, elastic to a degree, could be made in any colour and when a positive electrical charge was passed through it, would shrink to a pre-determined size. So, the outfit I wore started off as bulky trousers and jacket. Dress with care and make sure no fold or flap of skin is likely to get trapped, pass the charge through the Sim-Leather and suddenly I'm clad in an outfit so tight that it shows every bump or fold in my flesh and made my skin look loose. I was climbing a short ladder now, aware of the possibility, no, near certainty, that the dockyard workers were getting an eyeful up my skirt. I blushed at the thought and concentrated on making sure my feet in their towering heels didn't slip on the rungs.

This outfit, though, was relatively easy to smooth into place as my labia and clit were bare. I shuddered at the thought of my now ringed and swollen clit getting trapped in a fold or crease. I'd slipped into the trousers with attached corset and wriggled my feet into the tip-toe boot and "Wammo!" as the charge was passed through I was suddenly sculpted into a compact, sexy, pussy pouting bundle from the waist down. He found my generous upper half sexy too for he suckled my teat for a long time before lifting up my corset so he could start lacing me into it. This semi-clothed, pussy presenting state obviously added to my appeal. (If I'd needed proof that he found me sexy, the way his eyes widened and his cock jerked was it.) Thankfully, though the corset was integral with the pants, they hadn't used the same material to make it. He laced and tightened the good old-fashioned way until my waist was a hand span and my tits, crammed into the generous sized cups, threatened to overwhelm them. I had started to spill over and there was a lot to spill. Now he helped me shrug my arms and hands into the sleeves of the jacket with their integral gloves. Fastening it with a single button at the neck just under my collar, he made sure I was happy with the fit before passing the charge through again. The sudden tightness seemed to make my boobs thrust a little more, packing them deeper into the corsets' big cups. I looked down at my beautifully engorged breasts, admiring the tattoo, "Sweet Thing!" across the upper slope of my left tit and felt a masochistic thrill. He only had to wrap the pleated skirt around my tiny waist and pull and lock tight the flexible metal belt that was its waistband and I was almost ready for our trip.

"Master, may I ask a question?" I said as he pulled my crotch strap up that last fraction. He had passed the strap though my newly acquired clit ring before he did this so it mashed the enlarged bud. Enlarged! It was now too big to hide under its protecting hood.

"No. It's going to be where are we going and I want it to be my little surprise." He flicked my ring. "There, nicely available should I want to attach a clit chain to lead you." He saw me automatically crunch down to protect my tender nubbin as an almost electrical charge passed through it and I tightened up. He deliberately misinterpreted my action. "That's a good girl, keep clenching around your training dildo." I bit my lip with the involuntary clench as I had started the buzzing.

"Aaahh! Master, may I tell you something?" I already sounded breathless and it wasn't just my crushing corset. I knew I was risking punishment but I had to.

"Very well, Ginny Slut."

"Master, whatever else it was the doctor did to me, it's made me very -," I tried to think of a word that described it but gave up and grabbed the nearest. "Sensitive. If the dildo keeps buzzing like this I won't get out of the hotel before I start going orgasmic." He gave a short sharp laugh.

"OK," He touched the back of the ring he wore and the buzzing dropped to a level that I felt I could handle. Before I'd been to that doctor I would hardly have been aware of it but now the buzzing still felt significant. "I've been kind to you but you should be aware that from now on, if you have an orgasm without asking permission, you will be punished." He had his crop out now and slid it under my skirt and caressed my bottom with it. My pussy moistened around the strap and I knew that were I to look under my skirt I would see that my inner thigh had started to bedew.

It was a surprise. I had of course stayed on his heels through the hotel, expecting a Jitney to be waiting for us. It wasn't. Instead it was a slate blue flitter with navy markings and a broad yellow strip that made it look as though it were a present for a good little girl. I had promised myself I would be very good. Somehow, even this early and with little experience of it, I suspected that too much pain and I would not only come to enjoy corporal punishment but could also become addicted to it.

"In you get, girl." A human driver gave me a brazen stare and I felt myself go hot. I plumped into the deeply padded seat, making my tightly constricted up-thrust boobs wobble, and put on the safety harness. Other than for a lift it was too small a vehicle to have any of the sophisticated field effect devices that made them unnecessary. I caught the driver watching me in the mirror ostentatiously it was re-positioned so that I could be stared at. I blushed, realising my bare crotch was in view and tugged down the skirt. I watched the mirror and saw the tongue, it looked long and I could see a stud at its tip. It licked out lasciviously, wetting the full red lips. Her hair was blond and in a short crop, she half closed her almond shaped brown eyes and blew me a kiss. I just wished I could stop blushing and wrenched my eyes away.

It was my first trip in a flitter. In fact I had rarely ever travelled in a Jitney. Mum and Dad had their own pedicar and of course with each city sector having a full selection of amenities there was rarely a need to travel outside the immediate sector area. Of course I had been on a rail train when we went on holidays or when I had taken part in swimming or gymnastic competitions between sectors or cities but that was it. The flitter lifted straight up until it was way clear of the tallest buildings. I looked out goggle eyed at the panorama the city states presented. Of course the Eco laws made sure there was plenty of green mixed in with the buildings as well as that which clothed and roofed them but it seemed to go on forever, city seemingly sliding seamlessly into forest or rather jungle, for as much hung from buildings as grew around them. The driver kicked in the turbos and made the transition from vertical to horizontal flight with seamless efficiency. It was a neat job and even a novice like me could appreciate the skill in balancing the lowering of the power so that forward motion began to supply most of the lift via the flitter's aerofoil shape. See, I do remember most of my school tech classes. For the rest of the journey I forgot the lascivious driver, Captain Avon, my sluttish costume and my new role. I was just a little girl looking out of the window. It was a long trip but it passed quickly. I had been too engrossed in the trip and the sights to be aware of time. I wasn't even aware of him and I took it to be a kindness that the Captain let me drink my fill of the sights without distraction, apart from one jolt of the controller when I forgot to squeeze. That kick started me again, I rapidly went on to auto-pilot. (The flitter stayed on manual control all the way). I had scarcely even been conscious of my vibrating pussy filler.

The multi coloured expanse of concrete grew slowly, it was an indication of its size, likewise the geometric craft centred on each coloured square surrounded by shinning metal filigree. We were fully over a sea of concrete when we began to drop down. She made that transition seamlessly too. We landed on a virulent yellow circle of concrete at the junction of four squares, green, red, blue and pink.

Whoever laid out the colour scheme didn't have co-ordination in mind. The Captain spoke for the first time since the journey commenced.

"Bosun, excellent flight. I have to check something out. Stay with the girl until I get back. I'll be at least ten minutes or so. When I get back you can take yourself off and find yourself some coffee or whatever. Pick us up again at," he looked at his watch, "fifteen hundred hours."

"Thank you, Sir! Yes, Sir!" The girl had acquired a beret now and she actually saluted.

I sat alone in the back of the flitter and suddenly felt nervous and became conscious of the vibration in my pussy. Had it increased? I closed my eyes. I wasn't allowed to climax without permission, he had said and that horrible female with her long studded tongue was there to watch me. The cushion of the seat by my side gave with a squeaky whoosh and my eyes flew open. She'd removed her beret again and I was now staring at a square face, inches from my own, framed by a cropped thatch of bright blond hair.

"Well, Sweet Thing. And you are a sweet thing. We have at least ten minutes to get to know each other." Her hand had slid under my skirt and forced its way between my thighs, gripping the ring she found there. "This thing through your clit, Sweet Thing?" She managed to make the words sound scornful now.

"Leave me alone!"

"You don't really mean that, do you?" She gave the ring a half twist. The poor crushed tender bud didn't like it.

"Eeeek!"

"Give the nice bosun a little kiss."

"Let go, you bitch! Eeeeek" It felt like more than a half turn now. Her mouth was on mine and the hand not working the ring squeezed my breast. I felt her studded tongue click against the other recent addition in my mouth and for a moment I almost giggled, imagining us becoming tongue locked. It was a picture that my dildo prepared body and her working hands found attractive in an unwanted way. Even so I think it was the increased pitch of the vibrations that sent me over, it had a whole journey to prepare me. Her face was buried in my cleavage now, her tongue licking me as though I were some sort of lollipop.

"Jeez! You even taste sweet! I couldn't stop myself coming."

"Neeeooowwwwuuurrgghh!" I was jerking under her like a fresh landed fish, thrusting my hips, milking the dildo. I couldn't stop the roll of the orgasm. She sat back, still with that ring in her hand, watching me like a hawk as she jerked and manipulated it. Bosun was a calculating bitch. Nearly ten minutes had passed since the Captain had left us alone. Her eyes were round and dilated, her neck flushed, she was obviously as excited as she could be without experiencing an actual climax.

"Shi-it, bitch, thinking of you is going to keep me hot tonight!" She stepped back and that long tongue licked out and licked her wet fingers. "Your juice is sweet too. I'll remember you for a long time." Her eyes narrowed as she looked at me, I was only just coming down like a spluttering firework going in fits and jerks as it died. "You can make trouble for me, Slut, but not much. Long Voyageur captains are naval reserve and they may get a lot of respect but they have little authority outside their ships. All of us will be long gone by the time most of them return." She smiled a grim smile. "I may lose a rank but when you consider what you going to be doing for him over the next, - how many years? What does what I did matter? Anyway I expect to be acting as his driver until you ship out so you never know what favours I might be able to do for you."

It all sounded confused and I wasn't sure she wasn't bluffing. But I also thought that I might be able to get a message to Mum and Dad via this woman. And after all, she was right, in relation to what would be happening to me in the next five years, (I imagined a lot of wild things) and to the world in the next two-hundred years or so, who would give a shit?

Her cap was on and she was outside the car when the Captain came back. "Did she orgasm, Bosun?" were his first words. This deal the Bosun had worked out obviously did not included lying for me.

"Yes Sir!"

He smiled at me and said: "You know the penalty for unauthorised orgasms, don't you, slut?" I felt numb and humiliated in front of the bosun even though she had seen my orgasm run its course. "Out, girl!"

The bosun 'kindly' held my wrists as I was bent over the turbo pod and four sharp stripes were applied to my backside. As I waited for the first of them she whispered. "I couldn't lie, the seat you'd been sitting on was soaked with your juices. It just flooded out of you!" I had to count and ask for another at each stroke. When the bosun released my wrists I immediately straightened and the squirm I had been doing between strokes was immediately translated into a boob jiggling dance as I rubbed my bottom. The door was open on my side of the flitter and I saw the dark damp patch and knew that in this, at least, the bosun hadn't lied.

I got myself under control slowly. It had hurt like the very devil yet the kernel of excitement was still there. I felt that beautiful thrill that masochism and humiliation fills me with and I knew I would be wet between my thighs. That wasn't just down to my recent orgasm. Each stroke had aroused as it hurt, pain and excitement fighting for dominance. Perhaps just one or two strokes more and I would have come again or at the very least had me begging to be allowed to come.

Awareness of my surroundings came back to me. Each of the coloured squares that adjoined the landing circle was filled with gantries, machinery and equipment of all sorts. When we had landed I had seen nothing other than that. Now though, there were faces showing out of the dark shadows that were caused by the bright sunlight on the metal tangle in the squares, from at least threes sides. I was as certain as you can be with any bet, that even on the side hidden from me by the flitter there were workers waiting to catch sight of the source of the screams and moans.

"Come on, girl, don't dawdle stay alert. It would be inconvenient to clit leash you and lead you by it but I will if you don't buck your ideas up!" His voice was firm and commanding and sounded slightly angry now. The proximity sensor inside my controller had been set at about ten metres but he obviously wanted my attention focused on the practicality of negotiating the metal maze in front of us. I realised what staying close to him would mean and swallowed. My wildly erotic outfit in the main protected me from bumps and bruises and its secondary role to keep me warm was at least partially effective, if that is, you ignored a wet and chilled pussy and goose pimply bust and butt. What it had not been designed for, though, was clambering up and down steps and ladders, over pipe work and gantries.

The deeper we went into the metal maze of the blue square the more workers I saw and saw me. Stepping up and over, climbing up and down, I knew I was giving the dockyard workers the show of a lifetime. I had long given up any attempt to maintain any sort of modesty. It was a struggle to stay up with the Captain, my footwear, though non-slip, didn't make for mountain goats sure footedness. Climbing up another short ladder on to a gantry my foot slipped and I almost slid down it. Suddenly it was as if I had found another rung. I looked down and a hand was under my foot, holding it up and supporting me. A sunburned face looked up at me and grinned. I didn't need to guess just what he was grinning at and I flushed from butt to forehead. Scrabbling for the next rung I carried on up the ladder. Twice more it was to happen, I wasn't sure but I think they may have found some way to make my foot slip because there was always another hand to catch me and another grinning face stare up at me. I climbed the last and final ladder up on to a gantry and for the first time saw 'Sweet Thing!'

It was as though the breath had been knocked out of my body. Perhaps not difficult when you're as hard corseted as I was but nonetheless I felt stunned. From up in the sky, as you got near the ships had seemed big. Now, on that gantry, looking straight at 'Sweet Thing!'s nose she seemed massive. She crouched organic, manta-like, on the concrete as though about to spring up and swim away with incredible speed through the atmosphere. Her skin shone almost mirror-like with a hint of blue and I wasn't sure whether it was in the metal or was just the reflection of sky and concrete. Perhaps it was all three. "Sweet Thing!" His voice was husky and loving and I felt a little hurt at the confirmation I was only a toy to distract him and entertain him a while whilst he rested from loving her. Even a slut in a kinky world has fantasies within fantasies and it doesn't take long to form them. Stumbling along that final gantry way and down on to the concrete on which she sat on huge columnar legs, my awe grew. If she had seemed big, down below she seemed overwhelming. "Keep up! Keep up!" Had my fetish master turned into the White Rabbit?

The walk from the flitter had been hard on me and by the time we climbed the stairs into her belly I was red and panting in the extreme. "Hallo, Sweet Thing!"

"Welcome aboard, Captain Avon, I've missed you." The voice

was soft and vibrant and as I looked round the airlock I expected to see a beautiful woman appear and then felt silly, realising that what I was hearing was the ship AI.

"I've missed you, Sweet Thing. Everything OK?"

"Not yet, Jude, but with you aboard it soon will be. Have you finished dirt-side yet?"

"No. It will be a while yet. This trip is taking a lot of coordinating."

"Is this your new slut?" If she'd had lips I think they would have curled.

"Yes. This is Ginny Dunlop."

"Nice to meet you, Ginny." Can an AI lie? Or was she just being diplomatic? Some would ask can they really be sentient?

"It will be useful to have an intelligent auxiliary unit this trip, Jude." Was that how she thought of me? I wondered, an auxiliary unit.

"Yes. We'll be in the main cabin. Put the latest status report on the screen, please. The others will be here in forty five minutes." For the first time since coming aboard he seemed to see me as a person and saw how red, flushed and breathless I was. "Oh and have you enough supplies on board to make some coffee?"

"Yes Jude. It will be waiting for you." The deck was softer than the gantry plate work but that softness made hardly any difference to the way their jiggling, caused by trying to keep up with him, affected my now aching breasts.

CHAPTER 5

It seemed almost mundane to be sitting in the Captain's cabin drinking coffee. No plastics or simulated wood here. It was panelled with a variety of woods and I knew they were both rare and expensive. The coffee was good and sitting dressed and filled in my kinky erotic outfit, I had that feeling of skewed and, with that dildo filling me, skewered, reality that Alice must have felt at her the tea party. I shifted on my chair as I held my cup feeling my insides stirred with a ripe liquidity.

"I purchased her freedom when we got back and since then I've had a lot of money spent on 'Sweet Thing!'. Engines up-rated and the latest anti-friction coating. Refurbished in and out. The best that money can buy." It seemed silly to say he'd bought her freedom as though she were a person but I suppose all those years of relative and subjective time do things to a man. The corset forced me to sit bolt upright on my pussy so that the dildo was pushed in deep. I tried not to rock on it. In the warmth of the Captain's lounge my goose bumps had disappeared and my skin was moistening gently. I tried to ignore the arousing presence and concentrated on our conversation.

"What do you think of my beauty?"

"She's fantastic. I hadn't realised just how big she is. And she looks so," I groped for the words. "Lifelike." I realised just how silly that sounded. "You know, not like a machine, more like a living thing."

"I think 'Sweet Thing!' would be upset if you didn't think that!" He smiled as he sipped his mug of coffee.

"All the ships shown on Tri-D look sharp and angular, they seem smaller than this ship, more like darts than an organic being."

"Well most of those, from what I've seen dirt-side, were Navy ships. They tend to stay in the home sector and whilst they have to be capable of taking off and landing on planets, they tend to be in and out vessels. 'Sweet Thing!' has to be fully atmospheric because as she is a long voyage scout vessel she can spend months real time flying atmospheric." He topped up his coffee and mine. "They don't build ships like her any more. In your terms she was built a long time ago and she's big so that she can support me for years whilst we carry out deep space probes. I spent a lot of time hibernating but even so, with the suspended animation system I had, there was a limit to how much time I could stay that way. So she needed to be able to carry a lot of resources. But that's why modern scout vessels aren't as big as my beauty because their pilots spend most of their time in stasis. A colonization program as big as this needs a lot of support. She's one of the few vessels that can give it. She is really multi-role, as you'll find out. On the trip out we won't be able to use the stasis pods because we have to keep an eye on five thousand colonists and their supplies. And though now I don't have as big a crew as a Navy vessel," he winked at me (I felt myself colour because I realised that I was crew and screw!) " I'll go into stasis on the way back but she still has to carry a lot of life support supplies for a five year trip."

"How will you get five thousand colonists aboard 'Sweet Thing'," his smile wasn't exactly patronising but I had made him laugh.

"Oh they don't board here. They are loaded into stasis-combs aboard the drop ship with their colonization equipment. We mate with the drop ship rather like a pilot fish on a shark and control the whole thing." I felt a little silly but then I wasn't an aficionado of deep space travel. "The other captains will do the same with their ships but 'Sweet Thing!' is the only full scout ship, the others are ferry boat captains really, not scout officers so they don't have atmospheric capabilities." He put his cup down now his coffee finished and I couldn't delay drinking the last of mine. "I had better get you ready to greet some of my junior captains. They'll be bringing their pets and I want you looking your best. First, though, over here on your knees."

It had only been days since I had signed on and though most of that time had been spent preparing me for the voyage, I already knew what was expected of me. Compliant obedience. I left my chair and knelt before him. His dark uniform trousers were close cut to his muscular thighs but they were designed so that the almost invisible seams opened easily and fully under my Sim-Leather clad fingers to fully expose his already tumescent prick. Its length stiffened and grew as I took hold of its girth in my hand. I had practised enough with my trainer for my role but this was the first time with another human being and, taking a breath against the tightness of my corset, I lowered my open mouth over it. Well taught by my trainer, it was to be one talent that I would have to hone in the coming months and years. His cock tasted clean and almost astringent on my tongue, not at all what I'd expected. I remembered my training and as his now swollen head neared the back of my throat I swallowed and took him deep, timing my breath so as to not suffocate. Then, as I slowly lifted my head I set my now ringed and studded tongue to work. The taste seemed to work on me and I licked avidly, conscious of my own rising arousal. I carried on sinking and sucking, licking and lapping and I heard a mewing sound and realised it was me, eager for and needing my share of pleasure. Suddenly he grunted and hot sperm filled my mouth and overflowed. I swallowed the delicious soup and licked my lips, fingers wiping the splatters from my tits so I could eat that too. I was in heat and as I licked his lovely cock clean, inside I was amazed that I could find this still strange act so fulfilling and exciting.

"Good bitch. Let's get you set up now for our visitors." He cuffed my wrists to the back of my belt and undid the crotch strap, pulling it carefully free from the ring that pierced the overlarge and swollen bud that was now my clit. Hot and horny, it was as though I was being given a shock but by a sweet thrill and my knees wanted to fold. "Sweet Thing! A post please." To one side of the room a post rose from the floor and as he led me to it said, "Hold the dildo in, girl, unless you're told to release it." He latched my ring to the tip of the pole and I was forced to stand aroused and helpless. I had to work hard to stop the small but heavy and ever vibrating dildo in my pussy from sliding out, waiting to be viewed and I couldn't guess what else.

Captain Vernon was the first into the room. The girl who followed at the end of the leash was dressed in straps, boots and nothing else. Small high breasts with neat pink nipples occupied their own square of tight straps as did a neatly trimmed patch of pubic hair. Her long light brown hair was in a tall coiffeur of curls and with skin like warm milk, her neck looked long and swan-like. Knee boots, towering heels and hands in a back prayer completed her costume. "Pirouette for Captain Avon, Big Butt." With high cheekbones and neat red lips she looked like an ice princess. Her name described her, though not with complete honesty. If such a beautiful girl could be said to have a fault, it was that she was built like the majority of women. Well she was proportioned differently from me anyway as I'm top heavy. Big Butt's bottom and thighs were heavier than you would expect from one so slight of back but they were firm, well rounded and sweetly shaped. If indeed she were fractionally heavier in hip and thigh than the average pear-shaped woman it was only by the smallest amount. It was obviously a form though that the Captain liked and it was his prime target for her rear showed the marks of the crop and whip. I couldn't see if she wore a dildo controller but the end of a fat butt plug could clearly be seen. She was tethered to the same post as I but in such a manner that she couldn't straighten fully. Even as we introduced ourselves to each other it was as though she were going through a sequence of exercises to relieve the strain from her back and legs. Bending, crouching, standing with her legs as wide as they would go, anything to accommodate herself to the shortened leash. The last of these was the one that she could hold longest but it obviously embarrassed her to spread herself so blatantly for all to see. Dianne and I introduced ourselves. I'm not sure if we thought it would make the embarrassment less though why we should be embarrassed at all, when we had very similar reasons and sexual orientation, I don't know but that's people for you. The embarrassment got worse as the room filled.

When Kitty came in both Dianne and I went round eyed. I'm not sure she could be considered as being totally nude but she definitely wore no clothes of any sort unless you consider a collar and chain clothes. She was totally hairless and that natural ornament had been replaced by tattoos that turned her into a beautifully marked cat. There was no pantomime cat look, no black nose or whiskers but nonetheless her face had been made into a cat-like mask with dark patches around the eyes that gave them a feline slanted appearance. Full black lips and shading on her cheeks increased the catlike look, as did all the other markings on her lithe full body. If the markings weren't enough, her ears had been stained black, modified and extended to appear feline too and an implant grafted to her coccyx so that she was now the proud owner of a black tail that actually worked. The blackness of her tail extended with seeming naturalness between her cheeks to include her anus, vagina and lower belly, merging with her other tattooed patterning.

"I'm Kitty." She had been leashed to the base of the pole and forced to sit. Her tail wrapped around her and, holding its end to stop it flicking, looked up at us. As she opened her lips to speak we could see her canine teeth had been extended fractionally, just enough to further enhance her pussycat pout.

"I'm Ginny - his slut. I'm not sure if 'Slut' is my name now but it's the one he uses most."

"And I'm Dianne - 'Big Butt'." Both of us were reddening.

"My full name is Katherine but I've always been Kitty. I don't know whether Captain Burton took the idea from my name or it was just coincidence." She looked down at her own shapely breasts and touched a black teat. "I still haven't really got used to the real me." She looked slightly disconcerted as she continued. "It may sound vain but I think I look beautiful," The thought crossed my mind that all cats were vain and thought they looked beautiful. "But when I see myself in the mirror I keep thinking it's someone else!"

"Does it make it easier?" asked Dianne.

"I haven't worked that out yet," said Kitty. I thought about the question and what it implied. We were all compatible to some degree or other with our Captains, cooperating in fantasies we would come to enjoy, at least in part. You quickly became aware, though, of the need to separate the fantasy of your role-play and reality. The need to hang on to your own personality was essential, because if you became swamped by the fantasy of it all, you risked your personality and your sanity. Then there would be no husband or children at the other end of our long voyage. The gamble we were all taking was that if we were lucky, we would find someone compatible with us sexually but the emphasis would be family, all the imperatives of evolution, children, the need to build lasting relationships with their father, not just fucking and fantasy.

I shifted carefully on my high heels. I didn't want to jerk on my tender anchoring point. Two other girls were led in, I scarcely noted their Captains. One was a Nordic Valkyrie, tall and voluptuous in the extreme with white, white, skin on which black Norse runes had been inscribed. With blond, almost white hair in a thick waist length plait, the only colour was the scarlet slash of her mouth and the dark red of well developed teats. She too wore a harness like Dianne but hers looked as though she should have had a sword belt and dagger attached to it. The collar and cuffs that clasped her neck, joined wrist and elbows, (How it made her big breasts strain the straps holding them!) endowed her with the look of a prisoner of war, not a slave.

By the blonde's side was a girl as different as could be. Not quite as tall and as black as could be.

If Dianne had the face of an ice queen, this one was a Nubian princess with high cheekbones, full dark red lips and big brown eyes. She had a natural presence and carried herself arrow straight. Shapely but not overlarge breasts, a slim waist and a well rounded bubble butt. Her costume was her gold rings and chains of which she had a profusion: lips, nose, nipples and navel. She moved with a studied grace that the interconnected chains demanded but it became her as though she had always worn them. It was getting crowded and the two latest additions around the pole had scarce introduced themselves as Ingrid and (Would you believe it!) Salome, when the final two girls arrived.

They made quite an entrance because Geisha's master, Captain Clyde Clay was nearly two metres tall whereas Geisha, of Japanese descent, was quite small if with a very well endowed small figure. Little of that figure was hidden and she could do little to hide it because her wrists were cuffed behind her back. She wore only a waspie corset, stockings and high-heeled button bootees. She looked bizarre in the extreme because though her face had the beauty of a traditional Geisha, every inch of her body, where it showed, was covered in traditional Japanese tattoos, nothing was missed. It was bizarre but strangely erotic and beautiful. Penny, in contrast, could almost be overlooked. She had bright straight honey blond hair with a straight fringe framing a pixie face. She was slight of frame and dressed in a maid's outfit that clung to her figure as though painted on and showed breasts that were definitely not a little girls. It doesn't sound as though she could be overlooked but her Captain was as striking as Captain Clay. Just shorter than two metres in height in her heels, Captain Reynolds was a striking figure of authority in a close cut dress uniform. The breasts that strained the fabric equally left no doubt she was all woman.

The captains stood in a circle talking shop, ignoring the girls they had tethered to the single pole. We took the opportunity to exchange names and details. All of us were there for similar reasons, the possibility of children, a challenge and space to live and breath. Then of course then we got on to just what our captain had done to us. Kitty was the obvious starter.

"He had me modified like this in the first week. Of course it took nearly a month to complete, even in a growth tank. I cried when I first saw myself but as they say 'no gain without pain'. My sphincter had been modified as well to lubricate when I get excited and strengthened to take the action." She had a soft purry voice in keeping with her appearance and was speaking tough but blushing under her markings as she spoke.

"I think we've all probably been modified there." It was Penny, the little girl maid who in reality had the confidence of a queen if not the looks and stature. There were various nods of agreement. I kept quiet. I'd spent three days in the doctor's treatment cabinet and, apart from my enlarged ringed clit, 'Sweet Thing!' tattoo and rapidly filling tits, I could only guess.

"And of course he had something done to my voice." Kitty was blushing again. "I think he gives me something in my food too, to keep me permanently horny.

"Don't I know it!"

"Yeah!"

"Me too!" Rapidly the other girls showed and displayed their tattoos and rings but it was Penny again who topped it.

"Captain Reynolds has had her breasts altered so that she can feed me whatever the drug or hormone is in her milk."

That really was a show stopper. Surreptitiously we all looked at the Captain's fabric straining tits. The big dyke was giving forth to the others as though they were just menials, some had angry looks on their faces but my captain just had an amused look and cut short whatever she was about to say, leaving her looking extremely put out.

"Are you bi or homo?" Dianne asked Penny.

"Oh we're both bi otherwise we couldn't have joined the colonisation fleet. There's a general agreement to share us between them during the journey, they've a lot of games planned." This was a stunner that silenced most of the others though Salome and Ingrid looked as though they already knew. It was the Geisha who broke the silence.

"I suppose we can live with that. We all must be compatible with our captains." She had just a hint of accent so I guessed she wasn't just of Japanese origin but home grown as it were.

"Speak for yourself! I'm only twenty percent compatible with her," she pushed her chin towards Captain Reynolds. She took great pleasure in telling me after I signed on."

"Oh dear. Do you hate being shared with someone else so much?" The London accent in Salome's liquid gold of a voice was soft and concerned.

"I don't give a shit! I just hate being cheated and she's a cheat." We were all silent at this.

"Doesn't it even appeal to the masochistic side of your nature?" asked big bold Ingrid the warrior POW.

"What masochistic side? Oh she keeps me horny and I enjoy it but I'm in it for the voyage, not the sex." That left us dumb, the thought of five years doing something so against your own nature amazed us. "Any way, my card showed I could take it and I think she wanted to have someone would actively dislike what she forced them to do. So, like, dislike! I thought what the hell!" We all looked at her in silent admiration of this 'bolshie' slight girl in her little girl's maid's uniform.

In the silence Captain Jude's soft voice carried for all to hear. "Oh I had the good doctor use the latest nano-technology on her. Anal, oral or vaginal stimulation will work on her. Her clit has been enlarged and pierced and her G spot enhanced. She's also now in permanent lactation although the milk isn't really milk, more an astringent sweet liquid. You'll have to taste it." He had left the group now and was strolling towards us. "As she gets aroused she exudes pheromones that increase the arousal of those around her. That is quite useful as she's been adapted to like the taste of sperm and vaginal lubrication. Her body excretions too have been modified so that they always smell and taste sweet." He pushed between the girls and proceeded to pull my tits from their bra cups before folding the cups in so my breasts sat outthrust on their nest. Ever since I'd come from the doctor's cabinet Captain Avon had worked and suckled my teats at every opportunity to encourage the process. The fact that I was being brought into milk was one that he hadn't tried to hide. Today, though, for the first time they were achingly full and even since last time he suckled me my teats, they seemed to have grown larger still. He continued with his description of my humiliation. "Only another person's DNA will unlock her milk. Even if I were to put her on a milking machine it wouldn't flow unless I released it by suckling first." He turned to his fascinated audience. "She will always be forced to ask someone else to suckle her." Tilting his head on one side he said, "Shall we leave this little gaggle of sluts whilst we go to the bridge and discuss the voyage? 'Sweet Thing!' will let us know when it starts to get interesting. And in the meantime we can get some work done."

As my captain ushered the last one out I heard him make a last comment. "Oh and of course though the ship's medical cabinet is pretty basic, the doctor gave me a program for it so that the nano technology can be adjusted to fine tune or modify her body further. Within pre programmed limits of course, should I wish it." Stunned, I watched as they filed from the cabin, aware of the other girls' staring eyes at me and very conscious that the ache in my tits was really building up now. The realisation too hit me that I had been regularly tightening around the buzzing dildo to hold it in and that it had made me extremely wet and wanting.

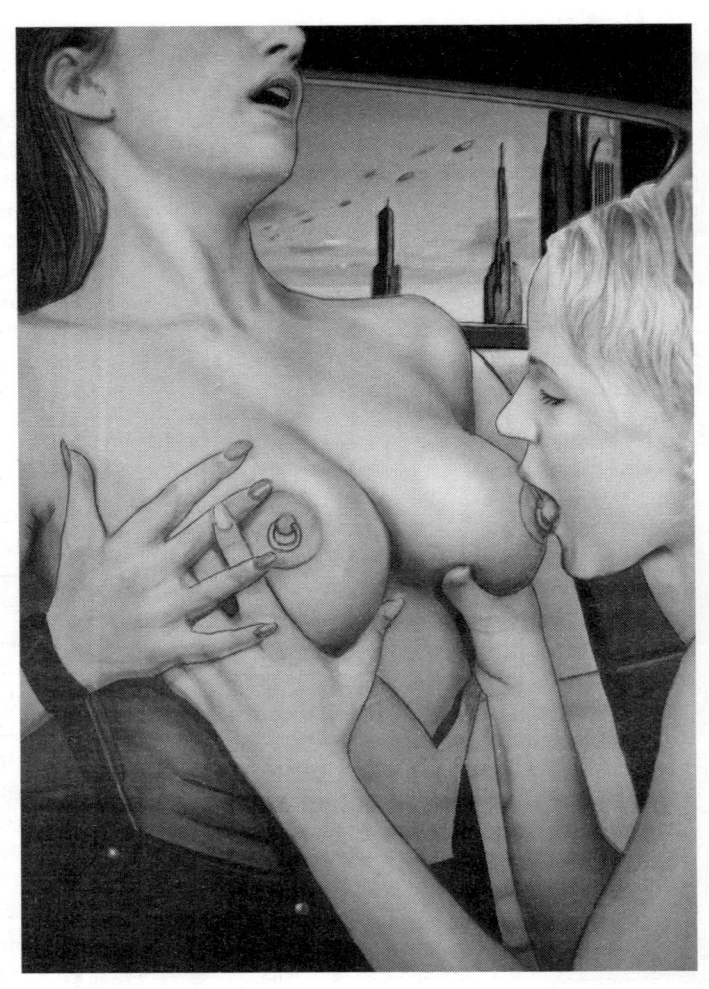

CHAPTER 6

The flitter was on auto-pilot and the bosun was between my legs sucking my nearly dry teats. On auto-pilot or not, she shouldn't have left the controls unattended. There was little risk of failure but even so the thought of us being untangled from the back seat of a crashed flitter slowed my arousal, if not hers. Bosun slid down my body. My wrists were still fastened to my belt and though my crotch strap was locked in place again, I couldn't stop her or the way in which my sex was aroused and juices made to flow. She was flicking my clit ring with her tongue and lapping them from my inner thighs. I hadn't wanted her attentions and even with my wrists held captive I could have resisted more but I wanted to ensure my message got through to Mum and Dad. So, I just continued to buck and push myself against her tongue.

Any person signing on for a long voyage, as I had, needed to say their farewells before they went to sign on. That process might take several weeks or longer but as far as they were concerned, their sons or daughters had already left the planet. The only communication they had was when they were told that the ship actually left Earth's solar system. No ship names, no Captain's name, no destination. There was a twofold reason for this. For the supercargo it was so that clean breaks could be made and parents allowed time to adjust to the permanent loss of their loved ones; for the Captain it was for his protection. Sometimes it was months before they actually shipped out. In the past captains and their families had been attacked, even murdered by parents blaming them for what they considered a living 'death' and dishonour. Yeah! Yeah! I know it sound daft but then, as I've said before, who said homo-sapiens are logical animals. I was about to deliberately break the rules and I wanted Bosun to help me.

"Aaggggghhh!" Exhausted as I was, I still came noisily and more juices flooded from me that the bosun licked greedily. Knowing that nano-bots flooded my system gave me an inkling of just why my body could take so much. They can't make anyone into a superwoman, what they do best is keep you permanently operating at optimum and shorten recovery time. As well as this, at a more crudely physical level, they can turn on and off localised growth of muscle and fatty tissue and can modify the hormone balance of the body in small ways. Lactation and bodily fluids, for instance, are natural functions so it hadn't been hard for them to modify me, or them, as they had done. Tits, waist, bum, etcetera, all could be changed easily. Obviously I'd read articles about them, it's the in thing for the stinking rich and Tri-D stars. Those Tri-D's show every zit or black head in luminous detail and they want to be perfect at all times.

Exhausted when I left the ship, with the aid of my little friends I had already started to recover by the time I made the flitter. That latest orgasm, though, knocked me back again but I knew that I had to carry on and do this. Rolling over, I made her change places with me, it was now her legs spread and my face between her thighs. Thankfully this was going to be less exhausting than climaxing myself. Her dark pubic hair was neatly trimmed and her little man stood pink and perky. As I closed my lips over it she bucked and jerked. She was already as hot as a pistol. I munched and lapped, enjoying her flavours, even though I now knew it was the nano-bots that had changed my taste buds to suit my new role.

For the journey back I saw no green scenery. This time the scenery was damp strands of black hair framing dark pink lips and shocking pink depths, surmounted by a firm pink and succulent morsel. I lost count of how may times Bosun climaxed. I was the one bound and seemingly helpless but it was also me that would allow no mercy. It was probably the first time I realised just how much a sub can dominate.

The alarm pinged ten minutes from the hotel and I released her. She was slightly bemused and confused as she attempted to fasten her working skivvies and simultaneously try to scramble, all shaky and damp, back into her seat. Needless to say it wasn't her best landing but we didn't bounce too obviously. I had to wait for her to open the cabin door for me and as I stood looking into her now heavy and sated eyes, I said. "Remember, if you don't deliver my message and bring back proof that you have, no more loving from me and you'll have to go fuck yourself!" I let my tongue lick out and show the metalwork that had so added to her pleasure. "We wouldn't like that, would we?" Passing messages like mine, whilst not exactly high criminality, were illegal and accordingly taken seriously. At the least she would be demoted, at the worst she could be selling her ass in a Jitney. Nonetheless she gave an affirmative nod and I was as certain as I could be that she would deliver it. She wanted more of sweet me.

It was late afternoon by the time I was dropped off at the hotel. If you didn't notice how short my skirt was and how hard I was corseted or that my wrist were locked to my belt, I could have passed for any pretty girl at a glance. That is, if it hadn't been bright daylight or you were half blind. I dashed my tit-jiggling way across the sidewalk and the doorman let me in without delay. It wasn't any kindness on his part; just that local by-laws made it mandatory that the hotel kept fetish and erotic behaviour in its environs to a minimum in daylight hours to protect the sensibilities of those not in the scene. A receptionist I'd not seen on duty before stared at me. She was all short cropped blond hair and red lips. It could have been envy, lust or disgust in her stare, though if the latter she shouldn't have worn the uniform that displayed her large whip striped white breasts with their small coral pink nipples.

"Miss Dunlop?" she asked. "I've instructions from Captain Avon to free you so you can prepare yourself for the evening." She came around her desk, fitted the key in the locks and released my hands before handing me the keys for me to undo the actual belt. I could feel the pressure building inside my bladder and decided I better not stay and chat with this part time slave slut. She looked regretful as I made my way quickly to the elevator, careless of what my flapping skirt would show.

It had been hard getting out of my outfit because the corset had been pulled so tight. But once that was eased I was able to use the unit to pass the charge that would loosen the Sim-Leather easily enough. Bathed and naked I lay on the bed, looking up at the mirror that was, I suspect, above all the beds in this hotel. I felt myself drifting in and out of sleep. It had been a hard day. I lay back on the pillow, my hands by my side and my legs slightly parted, totally relaxed, examining myself in the mirror. It was me yet not me. My breasts were already starting to fill again and my aureole and nipples had developed to the extreme, sized for adults, not babies. The flush as I thought about it suffused my whole body, for my pussy had clenched around its emptiness and I felt myself moisten. How much was that me and how much the nano-bots? In five years' time would I or anyone else be able to tell the difference? A feeling of fear filled me as my emotions played the game of taking me from one extreme to the other. Looking down at my teats to examine them closely, I saw just how big they were. My Captain had suckled them until I began to fill and flow but it was the girls that gave them their first major work out.

The captains had left us girls alone all tethered to the post and me particularly helpless. Now Captain Avon had told me, and in effect the rest of the world, that only another could ease the ache, it seemed as though the ache was the only thing I could think about.

It was silent at first, after the captains had gone and we were all shifting around our tethers, trying for comfort. I could smell the other girls' perspiration and excitement. We were all kept hot, whether by drugs or nano-bots it made little difference, the effect was the same. In retrospect it was inevitable that it was Penny that broke the silence. She was the nearest thing to a Dom among us.

"Shall I ease the ache, Slut?" She even used my slave name and didn't wait for me to answer her question. Warm lips found my nipple and suckled. It was a sensation that I knew would become addictive.

"Urghhh!" The sound from my throat was low and husky. I closed my eyes and another mouth took my other teat and the sensation doubled, "Urghooowww!" Opening my eyes, I saw a blond head that clearly belonged to Ingrid. A head was thrust under my short skirt and I felt a tongue lick out and flick my ringed and enhanced clit.

"She does taste good! And there's no way that this big baby is ever going to get back under its blanket even if it wasn't ringed." It was Kitty. Locked to the floor, she wasn't able to get to my breasts, so she had decided to test the statement that I was a human lollipop. Fingers, Kitty again I suspect, worked the dildo that I had unconsciously clenched and retained in my sex. They pulled it out an inch or so to see me struggling to retain it before they pushed it back in again. Geisha's mouth clamped over mine, with her hands cuffed behind her she seemed to cling to me by suction and tongue alone. Another face pushed between my thighs and a voice I recognised as Salome's spoke.

"She's so wet and tasty!"

It went on for a long time. Tethered as we were, restricted as to how we could move, we dissolved into a slow writhing knot of bodies and I was the core. The fact that they seemed to be killing me with cum had little effect on them and it was only the return of the captains that saved me collapsing with exhaustion. Of course they too had to sample my nectar and caressed and fondled me until I was moaning very loud and long. Seeing the state I was in, my captain eventually called a halt and, checking that Bosun was there to take me to the hotel, sent me off to take the flitter back. That was a kindness with one hand and a torment with the other. The crotch strap was replaced and pulled tight, 'Sweet Thing!' was given radio control of my dildo and I was sent out sent out into the yard to find my own way through the tangle of plant and machinery to the flitter. The torment was that if I drifted too far away from the right path the dildo would send pulsing shocks into my pussy. If I was heading in the right direction I would be rewarded with 'good vibrations'. Sounds easy? It was the first time I realised that 'Sweet Thing!' had a dark side, for there was a delay in sending the shocks. They got worse the more off course I was but they didn't start till I was well off course so that meant I could go badly wrong before I realised. Then it became hard work to get right again. It didn't help that the dockyard workers seemed to collude in sending me in the wrong direction and enjoy my discomfort and the pussy show. Eventually I found the flitter, near collapsed from stress and frustration. ('Sweet Thing!' would let the vibrations build until I thought I would climax and then drop them completely. I began to think of her as a malevolent bitch.) I fell into the back seat, whereupon all sensation from the dildo ceased.

Resting on the bed, waiting for him, I cupped a breast with two hands and with difficulty fed my own teat into my mouth and suckled myself. Nothing came. I could catch a hint of the taste but that was all. Then I remembered what he had said. So I wouldn't leak, my teats would only pass their milk if suckled by someone who wasn't me. In effect my DNA was the only key that wouldn't turn their tap. I imagined that I could feel the ache building even as I considered this. My dark aureoles were about eighty to ninety millimetres across and the nipples were sized accordingly. Were they indeed mine? They felt hard and rubbery under my fingers and a sensation, almost electric, joined tit and clit. I glanced up at the mirror again. Even as I watched the marks of my corseting begun to fade. It was the nano-bots doing their stuff again. I drifted off into a deep satiated sleep.

It wasn't until next morning that I awoke. Someone, the Captain probably, had covered me and I slept the night through. Alone in the room, the Captain had been and gone it would seem, I was forced to dash for the bathroom. Whilst there I completed my toilet, seating myself on the penis shaped spigot and allowing myself to be cleansed until I was deemed 'Ready for use'. My stomach still cramped when I was filled but somehow the process seemed to confirm that in my mind, I was 'Ready for use' too.

With no orders given and no tasks set I showed my independence and sent down for breakfast. It wasn't complete independence because my breasts were swollen with 'milk' and I ached for relief. They ached enough for me to want to ask the maid for relief but when she arrived she was gagged as well as being skimpily dressed. It was clear she couldn't help me and I didn't want the embarrassment of calling down and asking for an un-gagged maid. So instead I tried to ignore the swollen tender feeling and was on my second cup of coffee after the breakfast when the captain came back.

"Up, I see. Shed the robe." He poured himself a coffee and indicated his feet. I could guess what he wanted. Sliding from the robe I knelt between his thighs and unseamed him, taking his semi-rigid slug of flesh in my hand. The smell and scent of him seemed to fill my nostrils and I felt my mouth water in anticipation. His cock filled my mouth deliciously and I worked my ringed and studded tongue up and down him. He held out for ten minutes but managed not to come by pulling my head off of his cock. I was all eagerness by now and gave a little mew of disappointment. "You were a bad girl not being awake on my return."

"Yes, Master." This girl may be a sub and at that time inexperienced but she isn't stupid.

"You must be punished for dereliction of duty. A warning this time but top side it will earn you a lot of pain."

"Yes, Sir." I wondered what was to come.

"Over my knee then and remember to keep count and to thank me. You don't want to get more than you need."

"How many will I be getting?"
"Not a valid question, Slut. You've just increased the number."
"SWACK!"
"One! Thank you, Master, may I have another?"
"SWACK!"
"Two! Thank you, Master, may I have another?"

We got to twelve before he said; "The next session is for asking inappropriate questions." We got to eighteen before I slid off his lap.

"May I ask a question, Master?"
"Go ahead, Slut." Slut is what I am and what I felt then for he had made me hot and horny in the extreme but I had a desperate need too.

"Will you suckle my teats, Master? I'm so full." He made me straddle his lap as he suckled me and I worked his cock as though I was trying to wring its neck. The fiery tenderness of my butt fuelled my lust. I came at least three times before I could force an orgasm out of him and now temporarily drained, other parts of me had acquired a beautiful ache. He made me lick him clean and drink our mixed spending when it dripped from me. It was degrading, humiliating and delicious.

Today was to be the day I started to train to be a deep voyageur. Of course I was heavily corseted in black silk number that took my waist down to a hand span and left my breasts bare. Suspendered to this were black stockings and I slipped my feet into tall patent leather bootees. Thankfully I was allowed to leave out the dildo because he said it might be a distraction to learning. And so no other could distract me, he locked me into a close fitting chastity belt. Again as with most things he did for me and to me it was double edged. No one could get at me but should I get horny, there was going to be nothing I could do about it to relieve the need. And I was getting very familiar with the need. Over my corset and belt I pulled on a tight, long sleeved, 'V' necked black top. The top was cut just low enough to expose my collar and came down at the front and back to do up under my crotch over the chastity belt. Loops that went around my middle fingers kept the sleeves taut and the crotch fastening kept it so it couldn't ride up, keeping the bodice close and wrinkle free. It didn't show much of my cleavage but then that didn't make any difference because my breasts and nipples were clearly visible through the material. My last item of clothing - or submission, I should say - was a black rubber skirt that clamped my thighs together and hobbled my knees. I was obviously not meant to run away from my fate or go anywhere in a hurry.

The elevator was brightly lit and, as it plummeted down to reception, I was forced to look into the mirrors that surrounded me. I was panting as I acclimatised to this morning's corseting which was making my tits and teats move dramatically under the taut see-through material. But then my outfit was dramatic itself, it skirted the conventions about what and was not allowed during the day. It gave me some comfort that though the large purse I carried had little in it (other than a handkerchief, a communicator, hair brush and credit card) it would at least enable me, in the unlikely event that children were about, to hold it over my breasts. He'd warned me though that if anyone reported seeing me huddling behind it instead of displaying my assets, it would be the crop I felt and not his hand. The lift stopped and the doors opened. Consciously I lifted my head and strode through the foyer. I could feel my butt rolling and my tits moving in syncopation to the hard staccato of my heels on the marble floor. My face was flushing but I knew that at least this was home ground, where BD&SM was the norm. Outside the doors of the hotel was where 'anything can happen' territory began and I felt embarrassed and frightened.

The doorman slowed the action of calling a cab so he could take his time looking at me. I did my best to ignore him but made sure he got me a Jitney that had the appearance of a London cab of yesteryear. At this time of day the cloaking Tri-D image was like a sign saying that it would be a cab involved in the scene, powered by girls or men who were available for use but at least they would be blinkered and have a bot cab driver. OK, I would spend the journey staring at two bare butts but I could live with that if I didn't have to talk to anyone.

As the door was held open for me to climb in, I couldn't stop the ass wriggle necessary to do it but I suppose the doorman deserved the odd treat. I certainly wasn't going to give him a tip.

"Where to, babe?" The bot, its plastic half body sculpted and painted to look like a New York cabbie, recognised that I was female. It felt strange to sit and not have something pushing up into me. Two firm, well muscled female bottom cheeks could be seen either side of him.

"The Deep Space Training Centre." There was a pause as he assimilated and processed the information. I heard a low grunt and the twin cheeks began to pump as they pushed down on the pedals moving the cab away from the hotel.

"For a small fee madam can play with the ponies. Push the select buttons on the appropriate side of my column, it's red for pain and green for pleasure. The knob is turned at your desire for intensity. Please note that there is a limiter on the pain button for safety reasons." For the first ten minutes of my journey I resisted the temptation but after all I was going a long way away and these were crims. It was fascinating to see how they jerked and trembled, rising off their seats and showing the dildos impaling them, trying to milk them that touch more to achieve climax. I enjoyed backing it off that little bit to frustrate them every time. Of course I allowed them to orgasm when they arrived, though, as a tip. They were still wailing as the cab moved jerkily off.

The reception area was large and impressive. Wood block floor and cabinets showing models of various ships, tugs and long voyageurs.

"Sweet Thing! Supercargo, Gilly Dunlop." The girl was crop-haired and displayed a mannish efficiency in her Navy blues. "Ah yes! Safety procedures, use of internal and external suits and stasis pod maintenance." She hadn't blinked an eyelid at my erotic appearance. I wasn't sure if I was relieved or disappointed. "Follow the yellow stripe to Room 103. The course starts in ten minutes." And I was dismissed just like that.

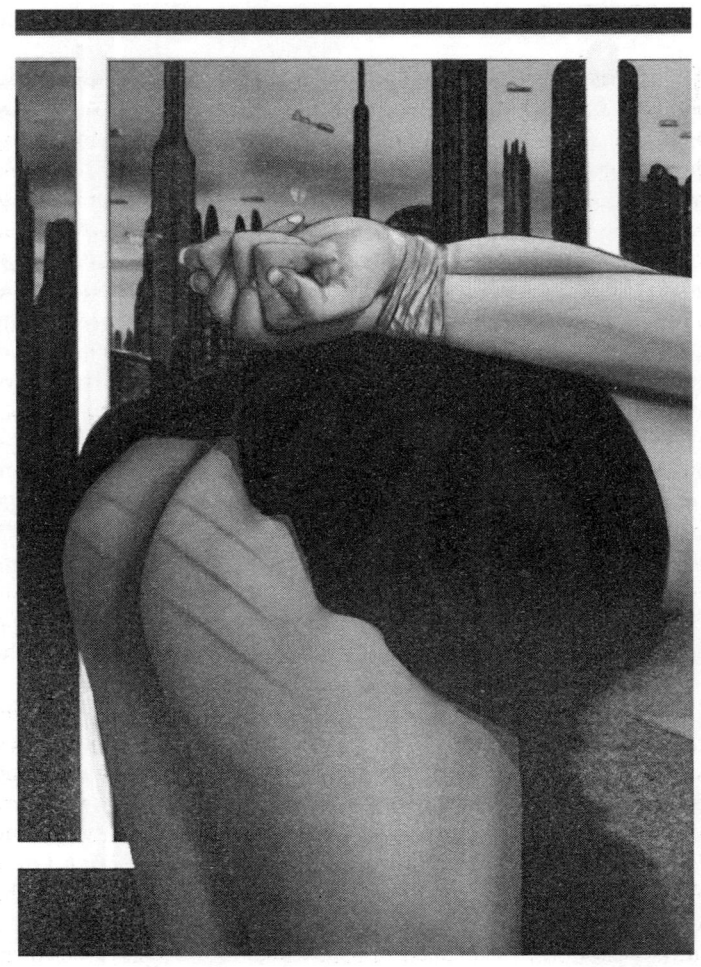

CHAPTER 7

It felt just like my first day at school. Supercargo Sex Slut and Slave or not I had to earn my keep in other ways too. Some courses would be safety orientated and others would be to train me in my duties as crew. I welcomed it for I wasn't sure I could last five years without some other stimulus than sex, though the way my libido seemed to be developing I wondered if this was strictly true. The thought of what that might do to my mind frightened me. A dozen of us sat at desks with notepads and pens to hand. They issued me with a pad as soon as I walked in. The instructor was a square faced stocky man in Navy skivvies with rank badges on his breast. What rank I couldn't tell you, not being familiar with naval matters. He was of indeterminate age, though from the gleam in his eye, not yet past the age of interest. Close cropped iron-grey hair added to the look of military severity, though he had a nice smile that reassured me a bit. Geisha was there, too, but the rest were navy or civilian straights. Geisha, though of course collared, was unrestrained and wore a neat, almost school-girlish outfit. Her beautiful oriental face could indeed have been that of a schoolgirl but her impressive bust belied that. And the way she moved! When she walked to the front to take up her pad it was as though she were cuddling a cock inside her. Perhaps she was, I thought, it wouldn't have surprised me.

"Now, class," His eyes lingered on my breasts. I wanted to cover myself but it was a futile exercise. Captain Avon had no doubt asked for a report as to my progress and behaviour and slouching would no doubt earn me punishment. No matter how masochistic you are, there are so many variations of pain and humiliation that he would no doubt find one that would linger in my memory and confirm future obedience. I wanted to avoid too much punishment as there was the fear in the back of my mind that too much would turn me into a subservient doll that revelled in pain without a thought of her own. What self-assertiveness I had needed to be hoarded. According to our cards the captain and I were almost too compatible and I had quickly become aware of the risk, I could see myself being overwhelmed.

"You manually write on your pads to reinforce the process of learning. The Navy is old-fashioned, though and so, though the pads convert and store your scrawls into legible script they also record all errors from punctuation, to spelling, to subject matter. You will repeat the work, hand writing reports until you're perfect. The pass mark here is one hundred percent. Space doesn't cater for ninety-nine percent. It bites you big time! If that appears pedantic or unreasonable, remember that in space, misplacing the decimal point can mean disaster." He stared around the class, no humour or lust showing in his eyes now. "The least is that you kill yourself, the worst is that you kill others." He turned to the blackboard. I wonder why they call them blackboards? The screen was blue. "Oh and remember, this is a Naval Academy and whilst here you are all under Navy discipline. Get course work slightly wrong and you have to repeat it. Get it badly wrong and you could end up serving lunch rather than eating it." He paused before continuing. "Or a whole lot worse!"

We started with basics first, listing all the safety equipment and its location on board ship. All such equipment is similarly located though homework would be to confirm precise details on our own vessels. The importance and newness of the experience let me forget my body and its condition but the human animal can take in only so much at a time so by lunch-time I was thankful to go with the others to the mess to eat. Geisha and I stayed together. I could still taste her tongue in my mouth and she was a sister under the skin. The others of our class couldn't keep their eyes off us and, dressed as we were, we couldn't help looking and moving provocatively. One of the Navy girls imbued with the spirit of feminine emancipation came up and sat with us. "Isn't there some other way you can emigrate? Wouldn't it be easier to work on skills to get a place on a long voyageur in your own right? Or perhaps you could join the Navy like me." She was a slim elegant girl with black hair, cut in to severe cap shape, one who made no attempt to look attractive but who managed it nonetheless. I felt myself bridling and the Geisha looking disdainful.

"One, my family doesn't have money like I suspect yours does." I could see a signet ring on her pinky finger, gold, which is common enough to copy but this was inlaid with a rare metal monogram and security chip. Most rich families wear these. Even the poor can look rich but those rings are hard to fake. "Two, I'm no dimbo but neither am I a brain. So the time acquiring a trade or skill and the luck needed to get selected is too big. And three, I don't want to spend my life in space in the Navy, space is a means to an end; not why I'm going deep voyaging." I sounded aggressive, annoyed at her naivety. She flushed and looked disconcerted and I realised that though naive she was a nice girl and actually trying to be friendly. I felt suddenly crass and boorish and tried to change my tone. "I want children. I'm of good genetic stock and genetically unmodified," (Nano-bots don't modify your genes, in fact they have to be stripped from your system before you can have babies.) "So though that's good and makes me attractive breeding stock, other than that all I have are my looks." I shrugged, shook my tits at her and saw her eyes dilate and her neck flush. "And my natural sexual orientation. That makes my duties bearable, even, if I'm lucky, enjoyable. To get me what I want."

"God, you're brave!" And you know? I really think she meant it!

In the afternoon we had a demonstration as to how a space suit should be worn. It was for internal use only, a unit for low temperature areas in total or near vacuum conditions. My suspicion is that it was chosen so that the 'straights' could get their first proper look at one of us. Geisha was chosen because her suit was ready for her. (Somebody could wear anybody's suit in an emergency but for comfort they were tailored) and because the suit had to be worn in direct contact with the skin, she had to strip right off. I'd seen her tattoos that showed below her slave collar but even I hadn't seen them in their entirety. They, and she, were a lush poem of adorned femininity. Her clit and labia were vividly tattooed and had been liberally pierced. Well-developed aureoles and nipples had been coloured a rich scarlet. The nipples protruded through bands of gold, slightly swollen and darker because of that. I wondered if they were slipped on like jewellery or secured by pins to her teats. The suit used a similar technology to that of Sim-Leather and their zapper unit was built-in, so that after she fitted the crotch piece in place over her swollen pussy and allowed its self seeking mechanism to locate into her butt and urethra, she climbed in to the suit and had it zapped to tighten it. These suits weren't just clothing, they were high tech and you could tighten these precisely to fit the slightest change in your body shape. Her tattoos were completely hidden again but she still looked like sex in wheels. I wondered if I would look as good as Geisha in one of these units.

That first day was like being at school again. By the end of the day, though, my tits felt tender and aching and I knew I needed to be suckled. I could have asked Geisha to ease my load but we had been split into teams and she was kept occupied by hers. Any of the men would have been eager to help me out but that was a route I didn't want and was too embarrassed to go down. Miss Elegant, Juanita, was in my team and she was the only one I might have had the nerve to ask. I'd noticed how she flushed when looking at me but that was still only slightly better than the men. As it was, the ache continued to build and I got hornier and hornier. Shifting in my seat and clenching my pussy at the same time as I contracted my thighs sometimes made my heavy clit ring jerk against the rigid covering of the belt. But that only built my arousal as it frustrated me. I tried going to the toilet, making my heels hit the floor like hammer blows as I walked to make the covered clit ring jerk and wobble but though it did, as did my heavy tender tits, that too only made it worse. When I got to the toilet, though the belt allowed me to pee, it wouldn't even allow a straining fingertip to touch my swollen clit.

When we were dismissed I moved fast, tucked my pad away in my purse and ran for the Jitney ranks. This time it was a standard unit and I didn't care that it was two heavily muscled and horny straights intent on lechery powering it, I just wanted to be back at the hotel. My tits ached to sweet distraction and my pussy was flooding, I was sure they could smell my arousal, they sniffed the air like dogs and I could do nothing! I was out of the cab in an instant and past the doorman as fast as my taut shiny skirt would allow.

I felt relief flood through me when I entered the penthouse suit. Captain Jude Avon sat calmly at a table, making notes in a pad not too dissimilar to the one I'd been issued with.

"Master, suckle my tits and fuck me!" There was little of the meek sub in the demand. He said not a word but grasped my wrists and, in a trice, had me cuffed and taut to a hook on the wall, one of the many provided as standard room fittings in this hotel. He shucked off my skirt and left me dangling on tiptoe. I couldn't shut up, "Fuck and suckle me Master!" I learnt for the first time just how much I had been made a slave to my own needs.

"You appear to have lost any idea how a slut like you should deport herself. I suggest you consider how you should ask anything of me and when you have decided just how that you should be, you should also decide just how you deserve to be punished for your current behaviour!" I had heard him but not taken his words in. I had turned and was humping the wall now, trying to get some contact that would bring me off. It was pointless.

"Master, may I make a request?" I was desperate but forced to think.

"Carry on, Slut."

"Would you suck my tits and fuck me please, Master?" I almost moaned as I begged for relief. Another time I would have blushed at the words but the need was on me.

"That's better, Cunt, but what punishment should you receive for your behaviour?" Again the crudity should have made me blush, especially because he said it like a name.

"You should spank me, Master."

"Ohh! I don't think a spanking will clear the board!"

"You should use a slipper?"

"Better, but I think the effects would dissipate too quickly."

"The cane master?"

"Yes! And how many, I wonder." I realised I was colluding in his game and my own punishment but I knew that the sooner I was caned the sooner I was suckled and fucked.

"A dozen, Master!" He considered and I continued my futile attempts to make clitoral contact.

"No. A bit extreme, I think." I wanted to just scream, 'Get on with it!' but I knew better so continued to play out the game until we settled on seven, each one to be applied hard and to an unmarked portion of bottom. The count, the thanks and the request for another had to be made clearly and without haste.

"Seven! Thank you, Master. Would you like to give me another?" The pain was sending shock waves through my body that felt orgasmic in its self.

"No, seven was definitely the right number, my hot slut." He undid my tight stretched top from under my crotch. It seemed to shoot up like a roller blind so my swollen tits and hard nipples were exposed and rubbing against the wall. The belt that had frustrated me all day clunked to the floor. Like a dangling puppet I was turned and in one movement he was lifting my thighs and fucking into my wet and wanting slot. My thighs gripped him like a vice now as his hands clasped my fiery striped globes adding to my lust. His mouth clamped over my man-sized teats and suckled. I felt the passage of my nectar and all was pleasure. I was in a deep thick orgasmic fog and by the time he had stripped one of my breasts he had come twice. I obviously hadn't been the only one frustrated or, I suspect, having the benefit of nano- technology in their veins.

"Urgh! Urgh! Urgh! Urgh! Urgh!" I stopped grunting when he forced my locked thighs apart so he could lift and re-position me to enable him to fill my ass. But it was only so I could draw sufficient breath to scream and moan as my other tit was sucked, whilst I was filled and fucked there. "Yeeees! Yeees! Yeeeees!"

We dined later in our room and I sat naked on a dildo stool by his side so he could fondle my tits at his leisure. My hands were cuffed behind my back so he had to feed me. My feet were locked behind the stool. I could rock and squirm, which I was doing most of the time, but I couldn't lift off the big beauty. My body seemed to be learning at a rate that left me wet and ever ready in its wake. He cross-examined me about the course work as he fed me and every mouthful of food had to be earned by a correct or corrected answer. My pudding was his cock, he pulled me forward so that I could do nothing save take his renewed penis deep into my mouth and throat. He controlled the slow and deliberate throat fuck. I took care to breathe deeply and carefully when I was able, the breathlessness aroused me and my tongue seemed to work with its own volition as I licked at and worked his length, tasting and savouring him. I was constantly aware of my breasts dangling against the material of his trousers and the way the big shaft had shifted in me when he tilted the stool forward, though I kept gripping and working it. His ejection tasted delicious too so that when at last I felt his cock jerk in my throat and he eased me off so my mouth was filled too I was ecstatic. The dildo shaft shifted inside me again as the stool went back on all four legs and I could not control the spasms of pleasure as I tightened around it. With a low, low, moan I came as I savoured and swallowed.

Eventually we went to bed and I was leashed to the headboard. I went to sleep quickly but in the grey light of the morning I used what slack there was to take his morning erection in my mouth. Again I confirmed my power over him by making him spend in my mouth then fed him from my tits to ease his thirst before we dropped off to sleep again. The alarm woke us and he lifted my legs high over my head and took me deep in the bottom. Any dislike of anal sex that had lingered from before my training was disappearing fast. He drained my tits then smacked my butt and sent me to shower whilst he booked breakfast.

I was corseted just as severely and my outfit was the same as the day before except that this time my translucent top was white and my large dark nipples showed more than ever. I didn't blush as much when I jiggled across the foyer to get a cab to take me to the Academy so that I could continue my training. My chastity belt was as firmly strapped as it should be, this time, though, instead of just concentrating my thoughts on my frustration, I imagined the arousal of those around me and the knowledge that any efforts on their part would be futile and wasted. How powerful is the sub!

CHAPTER 8

Captain Avon worked long hours to prepare 'Sweet Thing!' for the voyage and so that I could fulfil all my functions onboard 'Sweet Thing!' I too spent long hours at the Academy or doing homework. There were other girls at the academy who were also shipping out but not BDSM sluts like myself and Geisha. My straight classmates got used, to some degree, to seeing us in sexy or outright erotic outfits. However, the need for concentration and focus on our courses meant that for a lot of the time we had to ignore each other totally. Geisha and I were obviously still the centre of much talk and fantasy though. It was about a third of the way through my course when I really had to come out of the closet as it were and actually display what I was and what I had become.

My personalised suit was ready and though I had practised on the college ones, this was to be mine for the long voyage. So it was my turn to display it and my new found skills.

"Now as I think you've all absorbed as much of the theory behind the stasis units as you can, today we'll do a bit of revision on space suits. And as Ginny's customised suit has arrived, Ginny can be our guinea pig. Ginny, strip off to you corset and stockings and let's see how quickly you can suit up." Sergeant Khan looked expectantly at me and I found myself blushing. I had known this was likely to happen, all the students had suited up naked in front of the others and I'd known my turn was inevitable. "I hope the good Captain doesn't have to use your suit in an emergency, Ginny. Yours may not be the most unusual suit I've seen, we had a girl supercargo on the last course who had a working tail. That made suiting up process interesting! Yours, though, has six inch heels built in and he would have to make sure this adaptor was removed before fitting this on himself!" I blushed brighter still as he held up the pink rubbery material that was the crotch piece with its sel-seeking butt plug and urethra tube. On mine was a more than generous dildo addition. The picture of my master wearing my suit with its heels and both plug and dildo finding the same home made the men wince and all of us laugh.

He addressed the other straight students. "You guys have the standard Navy issue suits that are graded for build and size. Long voyageurs like Captain Avon and Ginny here are allowed a lot more leeway on suit design and what can be accommodated under it. For instance, Ginny will normally be corseted for a lot of the time, possibly with stockings too." He sounded so blasé about what I still thought of as something private and personal. "So, as you can't get out of a corset quickly this suit has been designed to accommodate that fact." He waved the limp red suit with its cream coloured V shaped front panel as though it were a de-boned body. "All suits, however, can be worn over clothes in an emergency, it just makes them uncomfortable but that is as you all know, why Navy skivvies are designed so that the crotches fall open at one pull." I hadn't known that. But it did make the reason for ribald songs sung about Navy men and women understandable!

I had scrambled out of the high waisted red rubber skirt that was part of my outfit of the day and shed the black see-through blouse, trying not to blush. It had been weeks now but I still did it at moments of stress. Geisha, as I expected from past experience, looked at me with interest and a little lust. Most of the male straights and not a few of the women's eyes were lustful in the extreme.

"Of course I advised Captain Avon what we would be doing today so he kindly gave me this." He held up the key to my chastity belt. There was no option but to allow my belt to be removed and offer up that rubbery monster to my crotch.

"Eeek!" The sensation of having my urethra invaded was made worse by having to accommodate the pussy stretching dildo and the butt plug as well. I found it harder than ever to look at my fellow students so I concentrated in getting into the suit, pushing my feet down into the baggy legs and into the shoes, hands through the sleeves and into the gloves, body and breasts comfortably oriented. Zap! Zap! Zap! Suddenly my suit was skin-tight and the mechanism that stretched the neck to allow me to climb though it, shrunk to a size to match the grooves in the helmet. The helmet was placed over my head by another's hands and I was sealed in my suit. Training took over and automatically I checked my air supply and the nozzles buried between my taut clad cheeks. Air was on and nozzles clear and unblocked so that they would mate with the standard female connectors located around the various vacuum and low atmospheric areas of the ship. I might be trapped in my suit for hours, even days and there had to be a way to get rid of bodily waste. For the first time

I noticed that my suit appeared to have huge red plastic nipples. Thankfully the plastic teats were mounted on the red suit fabric and not the central cream section. My face must have glowed like the filament of a beacon through the helmet. I flipped the switch that would allow me to hear what was going on around me.

"----- is lactating. She has to have some way to relieve the pressure. I understand from the good Captain that only another's DNA would normally release her milk but in a suited condition this is not practical so in this instance her suit nipples have been DNA coded so she can be mechanically suckled." Sergeant Khan could see from my red face that I could hear him. "Or, in certain conditions, physically suckled." He leaned forward, captured a stiff plastic teat and began to suck. I felt my nectar flow and I couldn't hold from pussy clenching the devices filling me and working my stomach muscles. The tight security of suit and corset combined with humiliation and embarrassment triggered an orgasm. Shiiit! How I came!

Khan kept me in my suit for the rest of the day and at some time or other I was suckled by all of them, even by the men I thought might be gay, men or women I thought purely heterosexual. They all appeared to appreciate my milk. So finally, totally outed and having no more real secrets, thereafter for the rest of the course, whenever my milk built to the point that my breasts began to ache, someone was always more than ready to ease my pain. That in its way was good but the Captain never again allowed Khan to have the key to my belt. So it became normal that by the time I got back to the hotel I was randy enough to be fucked by anything with a penis from horse to hamster. The next time I wore the suit, though, it was to be for real.

Bosun flew me to Beta Base, one of the equatorial locations where an elevator linked Earth and a giant space station that was in geostationary orbit above it. Again she broke the safety rules and let the flitter operate on auto-pilot. She used me and I her. Both of us came again and again and we arrived damp and exhausted. I, though, had been on the outside of my body, watching pleasure and being pleasured. At the height of screaming orgasm, the simple worn gold wedding band I gripped in my hand ensured that a disembodied me was elsewhere, thinking and feeling.

I had done what I'd done because I saw no other way to achieve complete fulfilment as a woman. (Now too I had begun to realise that my own masochism had also been at least part of what had driven me.) Mum and Dad, even as tears filled their eyes as I left, had encouraged me in what I was doing. They didn't like the fact I would sell myself to another human being for a night, let alone five years' subjective or two hundred years' relative time. With sorrow they accepted that life was a hard choice experience. Joy and love filled me and though Bosun wasn't its focus, it allowed my sexually and physically enhanced body to give her its all.

"You recognise the ring?" She held it on the tip of her finger.

"Yes! Yes!" I felt giddy with relief. "How are they? What did they say?" Bosun smiled to be the bearer of good news, she was making use of me but she wasn't a bad person. I suspect my nano-bot enhanced body was giving out with the pheromones. She was breaking the law but felt good about it and showed it, not realising her honest pleasure in that simple fact ensured I would do my best to pay my debt to the full.

"They said that they had got together enough money to go into stasis." She saw my gob-smacked look. "They said, don't build your life on just coming back to them but they'll be there if you do return or to know that you have achieved your aims. They said too that if you don't come back by the time they come out, the money invested will have gathered enough interest to allow them to emigrate, maybe visit their heirs. They might even be able have more children, they're young enough." The bosun added a thought of her own. "I told them, who knows they have might broken the light barrier by then and to make sure they left instructions to be taken out if they did." She leaned forward and kissed me twice on my cheek, placing my mother's wedding ring in my hand as she did so. "They sent that, too. Sorry I couldn't spend more time with them but you never know who might have seen me." I felt I had a thousand questions to ask but I knew she knew no more.

"I think we ought to get my suit stashed away, Bosun, and get on our way. I'm not the only one who's going to have a journey of a life time." I let my hand caress her breast through her skivvies and I saw her colour and little beads of moisture start out on her forehead and upper lip.

It was another journey where I would have a limited sight of the scenery but I didn't regret it. As I thought of Mum and Dad, I bucked my hips in response to her tongue going deeper still into my pussy and felt juices she desired and lapped so vigorously, renew themselves.

The Captain met me at Beta Base, 'Sweet Thing!' was now space side above it. "This may be the last time you see Earth. Rather than go topside with 'Sweet Thing!' I thought you should go up by elevator." This tough, often silent man who used and abused me, also never failed to surprise me. OK, so we had been told we were compatible but that didn't mean we knew each other or how we would interact. It scared me sometimes, the thought that it might be in my nature to want to be hurt and maimed. He never mentioned why he hadn't left me to make the journey on my own and go up with Her. I felt secretly pleased that he had put me, at least for a time, before his beloved ship.

"Did they explain about the elevator when you were at school, Slut?" His breath was hinting at the cold to come that would eventually force us to helmet up to keep warm

"The basics," I said and thought back to the teaching Tri-D. Alpha, the first elevator and its base, had been built over two hundred years ago so it was old-hat and boring to most youngsters, though the idea of actually riding it was anything but boring.

In fact the elevator isn't one elevator going up and down the cable any more than the cable is a cable. At any one time there are three elevators dropping whist three are rising, the idea being that the forces are always in balance so the effort of keeping the whole thing moving is relatively easy. The elevators themselves are only frames into which pre packed freight and personnel carriers can be slid. The loop never actually stops; the carrier is shot up a huge ski ramp until its speed matches that of the belt. A new, freshly loaded 'up' carrier is injected and the 'down' carrier with its load is ejected and brought to a halt at down a similar ramp. It's a curious sensation, rather like a flitter accelerating to about a hundred and fifty or two hundred clicks then going round a sharp corner. Disconcerting, but no worse than any ride at an amusement park. My master and I weren't in the main carrier unit that had all its space pre-allocated long ago. We were loaded via an auxiliary loader into the elevator frame's maintenance cabin. This was where the maintenance crew went when service and checking had to be carried out. It had few frills. It had air sufficient for one circuit in and out of the atmosphere but the small size and the rapid temperature changes tended to make it leak; not dangerously but sufficient to make wearing of suits, if not the helmets, a mandatory safety procedure. As I unstrapped myself we were already half a mile in the air and the huge savannah north of the mountain to which the elevator was anchored came into view. The slugs, not the insect but another metaphor for emigrants, to be loaded into their capsules on arrival at Beta Base topside, would see what we saw but not with such a gloriously uninterrupted vista. They had to be coddled in heated full atmosphere environment, so it was turns at the view window for them.

"Do you realise the link between the cable and the stasis pods you've been trained to maintain?" I hated to admit my ignorance but gave a shame faced shake of my head."

"The cable is a collection of long chain carbon molecules, wound in an intertwined helix, incredibly light and incredibly strong. If it were heavier the whole structure would collapse under its own weight. If weaker, it wouldn't work. As strong as it is, with the forces it has to carry, it would break. However any material will resist stretching for a time, naturally the stronger for longer than the weaker. The secret of the cable is that it resists long enough for a stasis field to reset it. The field blinks on and off so the cable is able to move and lift, like an old photographic film: we see smooth movement but it is stopping and starting thousands of times a second. The cable is actually fluttering in time, always occupying that instant of time before it has actually begun to fail."

It made sense, of a sort. The theory behind the stasis field was established back in the early twenty-first century. Experiments in quantum physics showed that certain sub atomic particles seemed to arrive before they departed. (Yeah, I find this believable, too!) It became clear that a sort of time travel was theoretically possible. If you can alter time then the other factors of relativity can also be altered like gravity, the speed of light, etcetera. We have learnt how to do this in relatively small ways. Local gravity control, stasis cabinets inside which time appears to stop, and not least the cable that flutters backwards and forwards in time so that it remains for ever on the right side of failure.

The Spartan surroundings of the maintenance cabin wasn't too uncomfortable and the suits kept us warm. And though it was going to take us at least twenty-four hours to reach top-side, the view made up for it. I felt like a flea wrenched from his hairy home to see for the first time the doggy unity of his world. The curvature was slowly turning into a globe and eventually the earth would become a rich blue with the whites of the clouds painting its sphere. I felt incredibly small and sickeningly homesick. We had come so close to ruining the cradle of man and even now the work went on. It was the renewal of the Earth's resources that was powering our expansion, too. Without those incoming resources currently being lowered to earth to help lift us out of the gravity well, it would have been nearly impossible to lift the loads necessary for the deep space exploration or the long voyage.

I leaned with my forearms against the Superglaz, entranced by the expanding vista, trying to see the sunset racing towards us but as high as we were, we weren't high enough yet. It was comforting to feel his hands on my butt. Vertigo wasn't a problem, we were so high but I felt so insignificant that I needed the comfort. My right breast was captured and his mouth was on my teat valve. I felt the drain and shivered with pleasure. It made me aware just how tightly I was corseted, how stuffed and full I was, how well trained I had become. Unconsciously I had been pussy clenching. It was a long day but one of delights. Halfway there and before we were forced to helmet up we sat in half G and ate and drank a meal from the hot box brought with us. To save weight for freight and passengers the elevators didn't have the gravity control systems that top-side or most ships have. We chatted like old friends but he didn't let me rest. He did everything he could to excite and deny me, suckling and teasing, pushing the crotch unit deeper into me, stirring me, causing the vibrations that would torment and frustrate me. He kept me teetering on the edge of an orgasm until I wanted to scream with frustration. We were down to a quarter of full earth gravity when I realised it was a game that a slave slut could legitimately play herself too. Now I began to fight my mindless arousal and stroke and fondle him too as I breathed sweet obscenities in his ears. It was a strange sensation; after we had to helmet up and with reflected earth light shining on his helmet it became the Earth I was making love to and not a man.

I arrived at Beta top-side totally rung out. Sex in zero or near zero gravity is a whole different scene. OK, because we were suited up we couldn't have man to woman penetrative sex and my master didn't have any relief at all, just frustration. But I fucked myself with the plug and dildo fitted to my crotch piece time and time again. Without gravity it was as though, confined by corset and skin-tight suit, I was just one erogenous zone, it was sensory deprivation in reverse. My body consisted only of overloaded teats, clit and G spot.

We were ejected from the elevator like a cartridge from a gun but it was less traumatic because we were in zero gravity. Thankfully my tight corset seemed to help keep my stomach stable and when our cabin docked with a lock, the Top-side manager, a little butterball of a man in tight skivvies that made me think of old fashioned Long Johns, was there to greet us. Captain Avon is a person of note, any long voyager with more than one trip under their belt is and he was an owner too. Gravity was brought up to earth norm and it felt funny to feel the flesh of your body settle back on your bones. The tightness of my suit and the corset under it had stopped my body changing shape too dramatically but even so my breasts dropped into a more normal shape and position as it came on. If gravity caused my big breasts to be less globular and stop them floating, it did no favours to the manager's fat little body. He was nimble, though, and led us to a shuttle port so that we could join 'Sweet Thing!' As the hatch closed I realised that if I ever was to return to Earth, this cheerful man would be long dust and, illogically, tears filled my eyes. The captain saw them and said, "There was a long march of native American Indians back in the nineteenth century referred to the as the Trail of Tears. Tears are part of the long voyageur's psyche, too." and then was silent.

CHAPTER 9

I lay on the bed looking at the ceiling. My naked reflection in the mirror looked back at me. By now I was well used to seeing myself in way-out costumes and bondage but for once all that I wore was my collar. That rarely came off and only then to allow something even more over the top. As I lay there I thought about my new life and the last few days. It was bizarre and every day brought a new twist of masochistic pleasure that deepened my knowledge of myself. It was a strange life built upon uncertainty. That was half expected, I seemed to crave it even as I dreaded it. Though it was the distrust of 'Sweet Thing!' or rather the artificial intelligence that gave her a sort of life, that really had me worried.

Three days had passed since we had transferred from top-side to the ship. Captain Avon had been immersed in the business of getting her ready to be mated with the drop ship and I had been set the task of setting to rights the chaos caused by the presence of dockyard workers on board ship. He had obviously decided that I was to take up and play out the role I had signed up for with a vengeance. We slept for a few hours once we actually arrived on board but, on waking, I was set to my duties almost immediately. My uniform had more than a hint of maid. Corset covered by a tight long sleeved bodice with frills that left my tits bare and available, whilst whittling me to breaking point. Bootees that kept me on tiptoe and shiny black stockings held up by six taut suspenders, a tiny skirt that left my ass half exposed and my pussy completely bare. My wrists were chained to my collar so that my movements were restricted and my mouth was filled with a large ball gag that was held and locked in place by a head harness on top of which sat a tiny white maid's cap.

"Now, Slut, you're to be another pair of hands for 'Sweet Thing!' to help her get all ship shape and Bristol fashion." I wasn't sure what Bristol fashion meant at the time and I stopped wondering as he bent forward and suckled my tit until I groaned. Equally I wasn't sure that, hobbled as my hands were and because of the shortness of the chain between collar and wrist, I qualified as 'another' pair of hands. One thing was certain I wasn't able to question him. "Remember, now you're on board ship, naval discipline applies. Slack or poor performance will result in punishment. She will direct you to your tasks and encourage and reward you just as I would with the dildo." I parted my legs to receive my fat heavy controller. Wetness had been immediately engendered as always when he suckled me and I had ceased being coy, (Coyness in a submissive sex slut is superfluous to requirements.) It slid easily into its slick wet home. Automatically I clenched hard to hold it there. His hands hadn't done with my pussy though, and he attached a fine chain from it to a mobile unit that floated on a gravity field to my clit ring. Fine or not, it felt heavy.

"Bring her back at thirteen hundred hours for lunch. She'll need to be fed and milked. I'll probably want to fuck her too."

"Come along, Slut, first I must ensure you are familiar with my interior if you're going to be of use to us on voyage." 'Sweet Thing's' voice was as soft and vibrant as ever but it brooked no resistance and somehow I got the impression she wasn't pleased that the Captain would be using me. She obviously didn't think it was a valid use. She managed to jerk my clit as she set off, making me gasp and jerk into motion. I caught up quickly in fear of a shredded clit. It may be considerably larger than it originally was, too large now to be covered by its hood, but even more sensitive than before. The small globe with its blue and white anodised surface looked almost like a child's toy but I was rapidly to come to hate it.

We went around the ship inch by inch with 'Sweet Thing's' soft sexy, warm tones, instructing, scolding and praising me via a speaker on the mobile unit. It was free to go at any speed and direction but hobbled as I was by high heels, corset and chained wrists, it wasn't so easy for me and it gave the impression of a frustrated bee, always buzzing and jerking, precise in its movements and stopping short of actual pain but always threatening it. The ladders and steps were particularly awkward to cope with but I did. The clit chain ensured that I was aware of my bum, swaying and rolling as I clenched hard on the dildo's fatness, struggling to retain it inside me. My pussy grip switched it on, causing a low background vibration to build, increasing my wetness and making it harder still to retain it. The gag, though, ensured I didn't protest. If I did start to slow 'Sweet Thing!' made sure I tried harder by encouraging me with shocks to pussy or clit via dildo or chain. In some ways, rewarding me for keeping up was even harder than the shocks. The vibration, transmitted by the chain to my clit, increased the arousal the vibrating dildo caused and made retention of the slippery shaft harder than ever. I wanted to hate this, too, because it ensured that after a climax I would be slow and awkward and made more shocking inevitable. But the pleasure was too great. It was a cycle that seemed to repeat itself ad infinitum, exacerbated by the questions she would ask, questions phrased because of my gag, so I could answer with a yes or no. The manner of my response would have been ridiculous if it had been anyone else other than me responding. "One squeeze for 'Yes' and two squeezes for 'No'!" She commanded in her soft hateful voice. The ache it built in my belly ensured that I had nothing to laugh about.

At last we came back to the Captain's mess just as the ship's cook delivered a meal for us from its metal stomach. I was hungry and exhausted, my jaws had long gone numb and my tits were painfully full. He made no attempt to free me, though, and instead refreshed himself from my breasts. That at least got rid of one area of discomfort. Near to collapse, yet how the sensations thrilled me, I experienced a sequence of orgasms that had me almost fainting but my body seemed to have no limits. Every cell of my body seemed on edge, even my teeth tingled. Satisfied with his drink, I was turned and bent over the edge of his desk. The dildo was pulled from me, making me whimper at the shock of cool air filling my hot wetness before it closed. Then the aftershock as his cock pushed its way into my butt.

"Nnnn! Nnnn! Nnnn! Nnnn!" My still half full breasts were mashed against the desktop and my ringed clit was mashed against the edge of the desk. My bottom felt so stretched, once I had hated the thought and feeling of being buggered, now my body revelled in it. And still I wanted more! "Nnnnnnnneeeee!" The climax was monumental; then as it peaked for a few seconds I fainted.

The desktop swam into view as my eyes re-focused and I managed to stand on trembling legs as he removed my gag.

"I hope you've had a good morning." My jaws were too stiff for me to respond and I felt dumb struck at how calm and ordinary he could sound. He actually seemed to care. He wanted to me to enjoy my humiliation and degradation by his machine. I worked painful life back into my jaw as I almost collapsed on to the stool by his side. Thankfully my sex was left empty as he fed me. Humiliated, degraded, my pussy still a-flutter from the series of climaxes that had been forced upon me, I found myself pushing my tits towards his hands as he caressed me while I chewed and swallowed.

The afternoon was to be a repeat performance of the morning until I was brought back to Captain Avon so that 'Sweet Thing!' could report on my performance. No fact was untrue but neither did they tell the whole story. In addition to the few actual errors brought about by nervousness, arousal or exhaustion, every pause or hesitation had been seized upon as a failing, every variation away from correct terminology was a wrong answer. In the evening, after the dinner that I served, I stood by his side so he could cup and stroke my butt as he considered my performance.

"Over the chair, Slut!" Un-gagged for once, I opened my mouth to protest but I saw the look on his face and realised he took her word above mine. Strapped tight in place, I could do nothing to resist, it was the tawse he used, not his hand this time and six of the best were applied with vigour. Each had to be counted and a follow-up requested. The six seemed to take a long time and my ass felt on fire. Finally, though, he was done but I was left strapped in place. It made it worse not to be able to rub my bottom or jiggle about. My red bum aroused him again though and he fucked me until his hot cum sent me screaming into another orgasm. I hung over the chair back, limp and satiated. I wanted peace, I was tired and momentarily satiated but satiation was a condition I had started to realise was only ever temporary.

That night I cuddled against his back and when I woke at about four GMT I was thankful that my chain allowed me to reach his night erection and took comfort in sucking it until I had him moaning for release. Then I took my pleasure in dominating him.

Day two was a repeat of the first except that 'Sweet Thing!' came up with an idea that was an expansion of the two for 'Yes' and one for 'No'. She thought it would be a good thing if she could communicate with me in an emergency, even if I was gagged. Have you heard of 'Morse Code'? Morse Code dates back from the days of communication via copper wires by means of short and long electrical pulses and was used by sailors on the 'wet'. Its quite long winded process but I learnt it in a day. My pussy felt frazzled and my tummy ached as never before by the time she had done with me. She would shock me with various patterns of short and long pulses, tell me what it represented and make me send back to her via the dildo. Even funnier than before' ha? Not if it's your pussy that's playing the music. Of course she was clever, she didn't report as many faults as day one but enough to ensure I got another six for not improving fast enough. It was humiliating to see just how the added pain and degradation aroused me. I could feel her optics watching me and noting my reactions. I began to worry just how submissive she and he would force me to be.

Today, though, was different. The Captain and I suited up ready for the mating of 'Sweet Thing!' and the drop vessel, then whilst he stayed aboard, I was let out in an escape pod to float free of the ship. Again he had surprised me, it was that mixture of dispassionate use and kindly consideration that confused me. At times he would step outside our master-slave relationship and treat me as a person with thoughts and feelings to be considered and at other times I was simply a toy to be played with and then my feelings and desires were never considered. It was my first time in space, no that's silly, I was in space as soon as I left the Earth's atmosphere. I had seized the opportunity, though, to watch the mating of 'Sweet Thing!' with the drop-ship from the outside as it were, as soon as he suggested I might. This then was to be my first time in space without the security of a ship or a top-side space station.

'Sweet Thing!' farted the pod containing this greenhorn and it puffed away from the ship on a low pressure jet of air. It was too small to have a stasis gravity field and my tummy was doing little flips, warning me that I might just be sick, unlikely as it was, thank God, as the air in the pod contained a drug to stop you heaving. It wasn't perfect and I was thinking of spending the next hour or so in a pod no bigger than a coffin (Not a nice simile) filled with vomit when the sight of the Earth and the drop-ship completely distracted me. A basic program controlled the jets that held the pod in a geo-stationary position to top-side some miles away. How many I don't know because I had no real idea how big that part, the Beta elevator, is. I knew how big 'Sweet Thing!' was, though, for she hung not a few hundred metres away. I saw jets of gas stream from ports and she turned slowly and silently to orientate herself and then small manoeuvring jets fired up. She moved slowly away from me, leaving me hanging alone in space, feeling scared. I knew, though, that I only had to push the panic button and, as the Captain had told me, someone would take over the pods control system from 'Sweet Thing!' and bring me in. I thought of her dislike of me and for a moment wondered for a moment if she had somehow busted the control software so the pod wouldn't operate. I shook myself, I was in an unreal situation and role but at no time has an AI ever killed or significantly injured a human being. She had gone as far as she had because of her knowledge of the game the Captain and I were involved in.

Shifting patterns of blue and white shimmered across the bright side of 'Sweet Thing!' as the Earth's light was reflected off her beautiful manta shape. As she sunk away from me I began to realise just how big the dull mass of the drop-ship was. Her bulk cut out a significant portion of the Earth's sphere but previously I had simply though she was closer than she was. In my mind what I had considered the massive bulk of 'Sweet Thing!' shrunk as the drop-ship swelled. It was an awesome sight. 'Sweet Thing!' did another graceful swooping pirouette and suddenly became a fish shaped badge on a huge thick oval. 'Sweet Thing!' had mated with her drop-ship.

My journey back to the long voyageur increased my sense of awe as slowly I neared them both. As my position changed, the drop ship turned from oval to circle to a fat line and Earth's light showed her true colours. The bright badge that was 'Sweet Thing!' had taken on tints of blue and red and sat towards the edge on one long side of the oval. The oval's mid section was painted red and the two lobes were bright silver. As I came near, my pod sunk below the drop-ship and I realised that what had seemed slim in comparison with her width was some ten or twelve stories high.

He handed his slave slut a cup of coffee and I sipped gratefully. "Well what did you think of the mating?"

"It was awesome. And 'Sweet Thing!' looked so beautiful!" I hadn't meant to praise her but she had been overwhelming and the truth will out.

"Thank you, Ginny." 'Sweet Thing!' sounded smugly pleased and for the first time she called me by my name.

"She's moving us to the assembly point to join with the other long voyageurs as we speak. Tonight we party and tomorrow we start the voyage.

I lay looking at my reflection, remembering the truly awesome sight of the other eleven vessels hanging in formation in space, like a small solar system in its own right. I realised what Captain Avon had said about 'Sweet Thing!' being fully atmospheric. A large portion of her size was the various drives and generators that made her so. These smaller pilot ships had a functional square almost architectural beauty of their own but they would never ride an atmosphere or land on a planet. 'Sweet Thing!' was the swan amongst the ugly ducks. Tomorrow we would all be off. My voyage had been irrevocable as soon as I had signed on, even more so when I reached top-side but now full reality hit me. I felt a shiver of loneliness pass though me but drew comfort from the knowledge that Mum and Dad would be there, waiting for me if I were to return. My thoughts turned to me and of the long voyage ahead. In the short six weeks since I had first visited the bot that trained me for my role I had changed and been changed a lot.

The girl that stared back from the mirror was if anything more beautiful than she had been six weeks ago. She was certainly more striking and erotic. Her skin never had white heads or zits. She never had period pains or mood swings. Her eyes hadn't had lashes as long or reflected the glint of near permanent arousal. A tongue with its heavy furniture licked out over full bright red lips and white perfect teeth flashed. The girl with her long black shiny hair was definitely top heavy. She lay on her back on a bed of dark blue sheets that contrasted with her creamy skin. Below her slave collar her full breasts, slightly shiny and swollen, with their faint dusting of blue veins showing through satin smooth skin, had fallen towards her armpits. They mounded high still, there was so much tit flesh. Large dark aureoles looked tumescent and gravid, there was little doubt that the long her fat teats would supply milk. Two fingers and thumb took one nipple and masturbated it as though it were a small penis. It was fat and rubbery and still a good eight to ten millimetres protruded through the girl's fingers. The reflection had a waist smaller than the naive wannabe girl's of six weeks ago, the corsets had seen to that. Whittling away at the inches, enhancing the curve of tit and hip, making them seemingly fuller and rounder. The figure I looked at turned on her side and her big gently aching breasts now piled one on top of the other displaying a dramatic outthrust too. Yes, definitely bigger, too big, but the bottom cheeks, though not big, had a bubble butt shape that at least balanced her in part and the legs were definitely long and shapely. The figure rolled back on her back and the breasts moved in rolling jiggle, settled back into position in her armpits. Now she parted her legs and displayed a smooth plump mound that was a lush pad for the action she endured and enjoyed every day and night. At the top of her slit an engorged and enlarged ringed clit stood proud from its hood and the wings of the cloak showed swollen and full between pouting outer labia. Fascinated, I watched a finger check the thick ring piercing the fat little man and the gleam of arousal built on those fat dark pink lips.

"Boing!" A gong sounded soft a low. It startled me back to reality it was a reminder that it was time to go to the Captain's cabin. 'Sweet Thing!" because of her program' couldn't see or hear into private cabins unless authorised or because of an emergency. I think that previously Captain Avon had allowed her total access but with my advent that had stopped. I don't think she liked it. I rolled over, my big aching breasts hung and swung as I got up from the bed and strapped my feet into a pair of tall ankle shoes. It was more comfortable these days than bare feet even though the ship's gravity had been set down to just over two-thirds Earth standard. Next I took the ball into my mouth and tightened the retaining strap. It had to be tight as slackness would only attract a spanking at the least. I tried to avoid pain though inevitably the right sort made me wet and sometimes orgasmic now. Next I clamped cuffs above each elbow and then folded my arms behind me so I could fit my wrists into the smaller spring-loaded cuffs attached to them. I looked into a wall mirror as I tried to wriggle and shrug myself into some sort of comfort, I should have known by now that was impossible. My big tits really did jut and there was no way I could shrug them out of existence.

'Sweet Thing!' was surprisingly roomy, especially since she had been upgraded to the latest, smaller types of drive, that and the replacement of the old suspended animation cabinets with the smaller more effective stasis pods. The cabins surrounded the central core and as I walked along the simulated wooden decking, it felt strange to be so naked. Corseting and erotic costume had at least given me some, if spurious feeling of being clothed.

"Ah there you are, Slut." We were firmly back in to our roles now and though it always made me feel wary, it also excited me. He suckled quickly as though checking operation and quality. It took some of the ache away though the electric thrill from nipple to clit made me clench but for once no dildo filled me. I felt strangely bereft and empty but it was also a relief to the overworked muscles of my pelvic floor. "Let's get you down to the entertainment suite," He clicked my leash on to my collar, giving it a little jerk as he did so. I hadn't a clue where he meant and I couldn't ask. The ache in my jaws was still there but it had yet to reach numbness. I could only follow him apprehensively and ever conscious of how my big unsupported boobs were bouncing and swaying.

"Tonight, the night before we depart, we're going to party." I could feel the arousal that the combination of bondage and his dominance caused but as always it was the fear of the unknown and unexpected that underpinned it.

Keep your eyes open for Part II to be published in January 2011

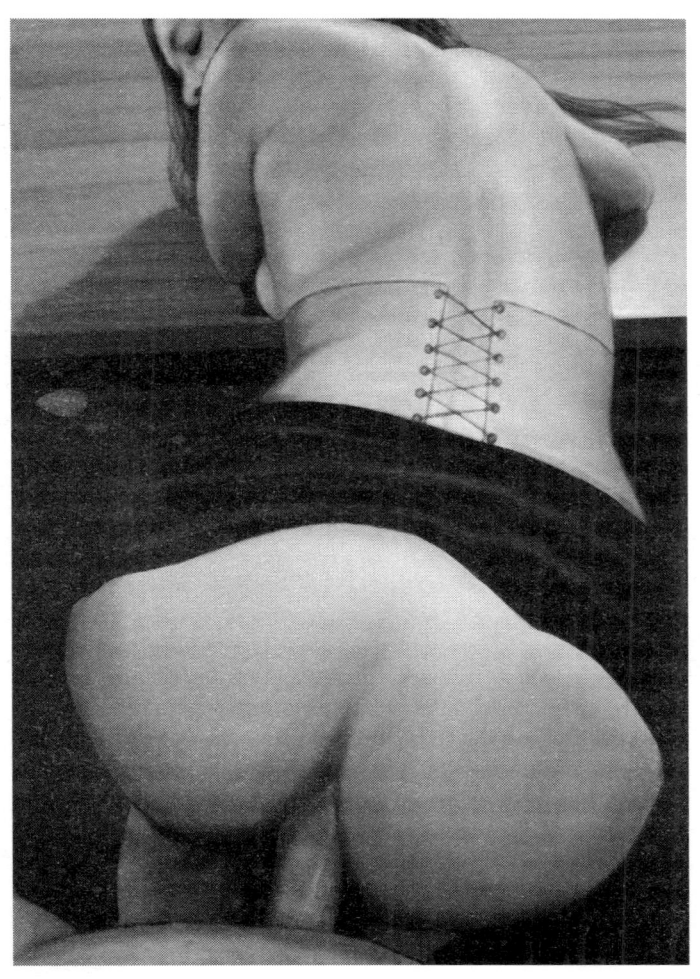